Moonlight Seduction

Stephanie Julian

Glossary

Aitás – Etruscan Underworld

Arus – magical power of the Etruscans

Enu – humans of magical Etruscan descent, including *lucani* and *strega*

Etera (pl. *eteri*) – Etruscan for foreigner, used to describe humans with no magic

Fata – elemental beings of magical Etruscan descent, including <u>*lauru*</u>, *linchetto*, *salbinelli*, *folletti*

Folletti – Etruscan fairies, only female

Lauru – Etruscan sprites who love to clean

Linchetto – Etruscan night elf

Lucani – Etruscan werewolves

Involuti – Founding gods of the Etruscans, those from whom all other Etruscan deities were descended

Querciola – Etruscan succubus, only female, induces fierce sexual desire in men and feeds off that desire

Salbinelli – Etruscan satyr

Strega – Etruscan witches

Versipellis (pl. *versipelli*) – literally "skin shifter": shapeshifters including Etruscan *Lucani* (wolves), Norse *Berkserkir* (bears) and French *loup garou* (wolves)

Chapter One

"Oh, now, that one has potential."

Sitting along the back wall of Lacey's Stay-A-While bar, Niccola Donato continued her examination of the condensation on her glass.

The rum and Coke was her second for the night but definitely not the last. Five, six more and maybe she'd be able to feign some interest for the group of men Tira Belludi had pointed out.

Her best friend had been sizing up every guy who walked in for the past two hours, weighing each one's potential as a candidate to share her bed tonight.

Since no one ever turned down the blue-eyed blonde with the pixie features and the body of a Playboy Bunny, Tira had her choice of men.

Nica could hate her for that ease with the opposite sex but why bother? Tira had been her best friend since birth. They had a shared upbringing, a common destiny and a bond forged through their entire life.

Fortunately for Tira, life as she knew it wasn't about to end.

Nica had until Monday. Then her life would no longer be her own.

She really should join Tira in her quest to find a bed partner. Who knew when she might get the chance again?

Tears tried to rise but she blinked them away. She was such a baby.

"Which one are you looking at?" Nica asked. Not that she really cared but Tira was her best friend and Nica knew Tira was trying to cheer her up.

Tira had practically dragged her out the door of their apartment tonight. Given a choice, Nica would've rather locked herself in her bedroom all night with two men named Ben and Jerry after her mother had dropped her bomb over the phone earlier today.

"It's time, Niccola. You're already five years older than I was when I took my mother's position. I've served my time. There's no man in your life, no children. It's your turn. You need to come home next Monday for initiation. Give notice at your job and tell Tira you'll be moving out. I'll call you later in the week with more details."

Then her mom had said goodbye and hung up.

And Nica had nearly hyperventilated.

"I like Mr. Tall, Dark and Sexy." Tira's voice brought her back to the conversation. "He's yummy."

Nica looked up and caught Tira staring at her with such pity, she knew she'd been awful company tonight.

No more. She only had a few free nights left. She shouldn't waste them drowning in self-pity.

So Nica closed her eyes and let her *arus*, the magic inherent in her blood, rise up, let it flood through her and fill her with power.

Then she took a breath to steady herself and reopened her eyes. The shift in her sight caused her stomach to roll but the ability to see auras made it worth the slight discomfort.

It was a Goddess Gift, not as powerful as her Gift of healing but useful. She studied the auras of the men, each slightly different but generally the same. They all had the pale blue aura of the *eteri*, those regular humans without magical powers.

She saw nothing out the ordinary in any of the men's auras. Nothing to indicate disease, mental illness or a violent nature.

Except for one.

At the tail end of the group, the man had his head down as he bellied up to the bar in the front of the building. The other men laughed and talked, their confident voices overpowering the other conversations around them.

This one, though, was silent, his mouth pressed in a flat line. Nice looking, but not movie-star handsome. Almost bland compared to the men he'd walked in with.

In contrast to his crisp, white button-down and pressed blue slacks, his light brown hair was too long to be considered respectable, brushing his wide shoulders. His nose was a little too big, his lips a little too full.

He was the shortest of the group, probably only five-ten but then she barely hit five-two.

Still, something about his aura... The hint of yellow at the edges made her look more closely.

From the outside, he looked tough, like he didn't give a shit about anything. But his aura... His aura revealed hidden pain.

So did his gorgeous eyes. Even from here, she could see how bright a blue they were, just not bright enough to mask the underlying darkness.

She had the overwhelming urge to heal him, tempered by the desire to get him naked and see if the rest of his body matched those broad shoulders and the perfectly tight ass under his pants.

Maybe she wasn't as depressed as she'd thought.

Still, she couldn't heal him. He was *etera*. An outsider. And that made him off-limits as anything other than a limited-time diversion.

Of course, all she had right now was a very limited time.

"Nica? Do you see something?"

Nica blinked, the auras disappearing, and she turned to Tira with a smile. "Nope, he's clean. Actually, they're all clean."

Tira's mouth curved in a wicked, sexy grin. "Ooh, goody. Now what about you? Do you see one you like? You could use a little fun, considering."

At that moment, Nica's gaze lit on the tall blond guy next to the man she'd noticed.

This one looked like he belonged on a movie screen, perfect smile gleaming, dark blond hair tousled. Too perfect.

His features were a little sharper, his nose, his cheekbones, his jaw—perfect. His eyes were blue like the other guy's but not as sharp.

This one probably wouldn't give her a second glance.

She wasn't beautiful, but she wasn't hideous. She had dark brown eyes and matching brown wavy hair, her best features. The rest was unremarkable, her Etruscan heritage evident in her strong nose, high cheekbones and the olive tone of her skin.

She'd never been the kind of girl men looked at twice. Not that she hadn't had boyfriends and lovers. But those had all been friends first.

She'd never picked up a man in a bar. Maybe it was time to change that.

The quiet guy drew her like no one had before.

He had issues. Big, messy ones that made her fingers itch to play along his skin and drink in some of his angst, letting it drift through her body and edge out her own.

She shivered, as if she'd caught a breeze from somewhere. Could be the air conditioning, cranked high to combat the July heat of an eastern Pennsylvania summer. It wasn't.

Her stomach clenched with nerves and that frosted her cookies. Men, especially *eteri* men, shouldn't make her nervous. Not a powerful *strega*, a witch from a long line of powerful women. A descendent of the ancient Etruscans. Human for all intents and purposes but her blood held an ancient and powerful magic inherent in all the Etruscans. That magic could do amazing things.

She should walk up to him and flash him a smile. She'd let him buy her a drink and when he asked her to go back to his place, she'd say, "Sure."

When will you listen, Nica? Always so stubborn. Always jumping without thinking.

Her mom's voice harangued her even though Carmina Donato had no idea what she was doing tonight.

Right now, she really wanted the guy at the bar.

"Wow, you're really into him, aren't you?" Tira nudged Nica's shoulder with her own. "Come on, let's go say hi."

Nica took a deep breath. "What the hell? Might as well live a little before my life's over."

* * * * *

Jensen Miller saw the woman approach the bar from the corner of his eye.

The blonde was a beauty, stacked and hot. Her smile could melt paint from across the room and she had it trained on Daniel. Looked like the tax attorney was going to get lucky tonight. No surprise there.

Jensen almost missed the brunette at the blonde's side. She trailed along behind and he only caught a glimpse of her until she passed the blonde and continued up the bar.

She was pretty with dark wavy hair and wide dark eyes. Not gorgeous, not like the blonde. But while Jensen could appreciate a beautiful woman, he'd been burned enough to know most of them wanted you to worship them.

He'd done his time on his knees. Never again.

He would've expected the brunette to stop with the blonde. Strength in numbers.

Instead, she kept moving down the bar. Probably headed toward his brother, Tanner, sitting on the chair next to him.

After Daniel, Tanner had the most notches.

But she didn't stop until she slid onto the stool next to Jensen.

Surprised, he glanced over to see her smile at the female bartender. Lacey had introduced herself as soon as they'd sat at the bar, her bright smile welcoming. And immediately tempered by the scowl from the tall, dark-haired man working with her behind the bar. That one promised retribution if any of them so much as looked at Lacey the wrong way.

Message received.

The two women seemed to know each other, calling each other by name.

He caught what sounded liked "Nikki" but couldn't be sure.

When Lacey set a drink in front of the woman and moved away, Jensen figured he might as well attempt to strike up a conversation. At least then Tanner wouldn't bust his ass for being a solitary loner.

He looked over and found her staring at him, a half smile on her face.

Waiting.

"Hi." He held out his hand. "I'm Jensen. Come here often?"

Jesus Christ, you idiot. Could you sound any less interested?

He wouldn't blame her if she ran the other way.

Not that he'd come here looking to get laid. He'd had a bitch of a day at work. Meetings all day, meaning he needed clothes other than the jeans and t-shirt he usually wore to the sites.

Tanner was used to ties and shoes that weren't steel-tipped. He handled the suit-and-tie end of the construction business, something Jensen hated. He'd much rather be outdoors, on-site with the crews.

Today, the school board had requested they both appear and it'd gone downhill from there. But that was no reason to take it out on the woman who had been smiling at him.

Her lips had lost their curve but her eyes had softened. "Bad day?"

His own mouth curved up. "That easy to read, huh?"

She shrugged. "I'm good at reading people. I don't mean to be a pest…"

She made a slight move away from the bar and before he knew what he was doing, he reached out to touch her arm. He didn't grab her, didn't restrain her in any way. But she stopped.

"You're not a pest. I could use the company. And what man would turn away a pretty woman?"

Her lopsided smile said she wasn't buying the pretty woman comment. But the more he stared at her, the more he realized just how pretty she was.

What did she see in a bad-tempered idiot like him?

"So tell me about your bad day, Jensen. I'm Nica, by the way."

She held out a small, slim hand. No rings. He took it automatically and didn't release her right away, caught in the warmth of her dark eyes. She seemed genuinely interested in him and he couldn't help but wonder what she was after.

He shook the thought out of his head. Hell, he needed to get over himself. Not every woman had ulterior motives for talking to a guy.

"Well, to begin with, I'm dressed like the rest of these yahoos, so that's sure to set me off right away."

She laughed, a rich, deep sound that hit him low in the gut.

"And second, I spent the day cooped up inside talking."

"So you're a man of action, not words?"

He nodded. "My brother can say a few words and have an entire school board eating out of his hand. I say one thing and piss them all off."

She laughed again and his cock began to harden. Damn it, now he really wished he'd worn jeans. They hid an erection better than these flimsy pants.

"What do you do for a living, Jensen?" She picked up her glass and took a drink, licking away a drop of liquid from her lip and making his mouth dry with lust.

He cleared his throat. "My brother and I run Miller Construction. He's CFO. I'm COO."

"And what exactly does that mean?"

"It means he handles the money and I handle the actual work. We each have our strengths."

"Sounds like you work well together."

Oh baby, if you only knew.

And maybe, if he was very lucky and didn't scare her away, she'd find out just how well he and Tanner worked together.

Her head cocked to the side when he didn't comment right away, that lopsided smile returning.

His body temperature rose as his erection hardened another degree. And he felt more of his stress slide away.

Maybe this day wouldn't be a total bust after all.

* * * * *

"So are you going to introduce me to the beautiful woman, Jensen, or keep her to yourself all night?"

Nica glanced up to find herself staring into the pale blue eyes of the blond man sitting next to Jensen at the bar.

She didn't know how long she and Jensen had been talking but she was surprised at how easy it'd been. She'd never considered herself good at small talk, and she certainly hadn't come out tonight looking for conversation.

She'd wanted to lose herself in alcohol. Not pretty but it was the truth.

Then she'd met Jensen and they'd hit it off.

It'd taken her a little while to get a smile out of him and, when he finally grinned, she decided she needed to rethink her assessment that he wasn't the most handsome man in the room.

That smile popped up now as Jensen rolled his eyes and pointed his thumb over his shoulder.

"Nica, my brother, Tanner."

Tanner reached around Jensen to offer his hand. She took it, startled to feel the same flash of attraction she'd felt the first time she'd touched Jensen.

Not that she didn't find Tanner attractive. He was.

"Older brother," Tanner added with a grin.

Jensen snorted. "By fifteen minutes. He has a slight ego problem."

Her eyes widened as she looked back and forth between the brothers. "You're twins?"

"Unfortunately, yes." Tanner sighed theatrically, a casual arm thrown around his brother's shoulders. "Though he barely admits to being related most of the time."

She could see the resemblance now, as they stood side by side. It was there in the shape of their nose and eyes, even as everything else about them was different.

"And why's that?" she asked.

"Because he's an idiot, that's why." Jensen shook his head but Nica heard the smile in his voice.

They had a true affection for each other, Nica realized.

She had no siblings, though growing up in the small village owned by the *boschetta* on the outskirts of the city, she had what amounted to familial ties with the children born to the *boschetta*. Like Tira, still holding court with the three other men.

Tanner had been dancing to Tira's tune until just a few minutes ago. Not that Nica didn't appreciate the attention from another handsome guy. She just didn't want to be a bone of contention between the brothers.

Would this turn into a pissing contest? Some women might like that. Not her.

But she saw nothing in either man's expression to indicate jealousy. In fact, as they continued to talk, it became apparent that they actually liked each other.

But they didn't exclude her the way some guys might when they talked to each other.

They discussed the public school system and the failing infrastructure. Since she'd never gone to a public school, she nodded at all the appropriate times and tried not to sound as if she'd had an unusual upbringing.

When they somehow got onto the subject of global warming and people's general disregard for the earth's waning resources, she found both men good listeners who never made her feel her opinions were stupid or wrong. They argued about the state of the union and whether or not hockey or football was the toughest sport.

The men moved closer as the night went on, surrounding her, filling her field of vision until she saw only them. The heat of their bodies felt like the sun on her skin. She drew in warm male scents, the flesh between her legs growing more wet and swollen with each passing minute.

And when Lacey, the bar owner, announced last call, Nica looked at Jensen then Tanner and saw the same question in both their gazes.

At twenty-six, Nica was by no means sheltered. She'd grown up in a community where sex was a vital part of their rituals, not a dirty deed locked away behind closed doors.

Sex was natural. It produced energy to power magic and that was something encouraged by the *boschetta*. She'd been taught how to take partners to enhance specific spells.

But she'd never had two.

And that was their question. They didn't have to say it aloud. It'd been an undercurrent in the conversation since Tanner had joined them.

She'd been considering the possibilities.

And since this could be her last free night for…well, for a very long time, she wanted it to be a night to remember.

* * * * *

Tanner watched Nica closely, wondering if she was going to say yes.

Even though neither he nor Jensen had asked her to go home— with both of them.

He couldn't tell if the look in her eyes was confusion or contemplation. Couldn't tell if the look she leveled on Jensen meant she was hoping she was wrong and he would ask her to go home only with him. Or if she was going to run screaming in the opposite direction.

He couldn't say he'd given her more than a cursory glance when she'd walked over to the bar with the blonde. Busty, beautiful Tira had immediately caught his eye, even though he hadn't come out tonight looking for a diversion other than a few cold beers.

When Tira had made it clear she was interested in Daniel, he'd laughed and smiled at the appropriate times, not too upset that she'd passed him over.

His mind had been on the meeting today. They still had some damage control to take care of and he knew how much Jensen hated dealing with suits. After that meeting, he hadn't expected Jensen to come along to the bar. But his brother had been wound tight and Tanner thought Jensen could stand to let off some steam.

Then Nica had walked up to Jensen and Tanner had seen something in his brother's expression that hadn't been there for a while.

Hunger.

He'd been worried about Jensen after that deal with Penny. That bitch had made his brother doubt himself and that was something Tanner had never thought he'd see.

Not rock-solid Jensen who never faltered, never failed.

Jensen had fallen harder for Penny than he'd let on and Tanner blamed himself for not seeing the problem before it blew into a crisis. He'd been blinded by a woman with an ulterior motive.

Tonight, he hadn't picked up any skanky vibes from Nica and he'd been watching. Closely.

Jensen had guided the conversation all night. If he'd picked up something from Nica, he would've flashed Tanner the look. The one that said, "Get me the hell out of here."

Instead, Jensen had talked. And talked.

"Do you live close by?"

Jensen's quiet question drew Tanner back to the conversation as he listened for Nica's response.

"My friend and I share an apartment on South Fifth Street," she said. "Not far from the French-Italian bakery. What about you? Do you live in the city?"

"No, we're in Wyomissing. Tanner and I are rehabbing an old cottage up the road from the Reading Museum."

Tanner watched as Nica nodded, those dark eyes mesmerizing.

Heat sizzled through his blood, straight to his cock. He hadn't felt this excited about a woman in months and he couldn't help but wonder if the reason he wanted her was because Jensen did. His brother had sworn off women the past few months as they'd both been swamped by work.

With the economy still not on solid ground, new construction wasn't high on anybody's list. But they'd been lucky lately and had landed some school renovation projects that would keep their company rolling for a while. So far, they'd weathered the economic downturn. They couldn't afford not to. Too many people depended on them.

He and Jensen couldn't afford to be at odds now. Especially over a woman. If this woman only wanted Jensen, he'd step away, no harm no foul.

If she made a play for him through Jensen—like Penny—he'd walk away as far and as fast as he could. He never again wanted to live through the months like they'd had last year.

His relationship with Jensen was more important than any fleeting fuck with a woman.

"Would you like to see our house, Nica?"

Her expression showed no hint of her thoughts, only that same heated interest, whether she looked at him or Jensen.

Did she actually understand what Jensen was asking? Did she really know what they wanted?

Nica's heart began to beat a hard and fast pace.

As if these two gorgeous men were already touching her body, making her respond, making her thighs quiver and her womb tighten with lust.

They both wanted her and if she went home with them, they'd both have her. Which excited her more than she could have ever imagined.

Maybe it was the fact that she was about to give her life over to the *boschetta* that made her feel so reckless.

Maybe it was the fact that she hadn't been given a choice in her life. She'd been born to fulfill a role. Her entire life had been spent learning all she needed to know to take on that role.

She'd never questioned, never complained. She'd known when she and Tira had taken the apartment in town last year that it'd be temporary. That eventually she'd return to the *boschetta* and take her mother's place.

She just hadn't expected it to be this soon.

The day she returned to the *boschetta*, her life would be consumed by duty, her world constrained to the confines of the small village the *boschetta* owned in the hills of Brecknock Township.

She looked first at Jensen then at Tanner.

"I'd love to see your home."

She didn't rush the words but the breathless quality of her voice gave away her excitement.

Tanner's mouth split in a wide grin, his eyes narrowing down to slices of pale blue.

Jensen didn't smile. Instead he put his hand over hers lying on the bar. His skin burned hot, his gaze going molten. And her chest tightened to the point she could barely breathe.

"Where are you parked?" Jensen asked.

"I came with Tira."

Jensen's eyes flared ice-blue, not cold but hot, like the flame of a blowtorch. Flipping her hand, he laced their fingers together. It was the first time he'd really touched her and the sensation nearly overloaded her already burning nervous system.

"My car's out front," he said. "Let me give you our address to give to your friend."

Her lips curved in a smile as her thighs tightened and her pussy clenched. Hell, she was leaving with two men she'd only met hours before and hadn't even thought to ask where they were going.

So you're really going through with this. Are you nuts?

No, she wasn't crazy. Maybe a little reckless yes, but she was going to take what she wanted, while she could. Today, her life was still her own.

Next week…

Jensen's hand loosened around hers, as if he'd read her thoughts and misinterpreted her feelings. He didn't want her to feel trapped. Tanner actually leaned away from her the slightest bit.

She couldn't help but smile. "Let me get my purse."

She slid off the stool, prompting Jensen to do the same. He took the business card Tanner fished out of his back pocket and wrote something on the back with the pen in his front pocket.

Tanner pointed at it as Jensen handed it to her. "That's our address. The number on the front rings our cells as well as the house."

"I'll just let Tira know I'm leaving."

Catching Tira's eye as she passed, they met back at their table, where they'd left their purses.

"So you're going home with him?" Tira practically glowed with excitement.

"I'm going home with both of them." She handed her friend the card. "They want you to have this. Their address is on the back."

Tira's eyes widened until Nica thought they might fall out of her head. Then she flashed a look at Tanner and Jensen, standing by the bar. "No way."

Nica couldn't tell whether Tira was shocked or envious. Then Tira started to grin. "Whoa, Nica. I want details tomorrow. Lots and lots of details." Then she hesitated. "But…"

Nica glanced up from her retrieving her purse. "But what?"

Tira glanced at the men again then looked at Nica. Nica knew her friend was trying to catch a vision, to see into her future. Then Tira shook her head and smiled. "Nothing. I'm not seeing anything. Have a good time, Nica. Enjoy yourself."

Enjoy yourself.

Those words continued to circulate through her head as she walked back to the brothers, Tanner's smile easy and open, Jensen's gaze intense.

Doubt tried to settle into her chest but she moved forward, her gaze caught on Jensen's.

"Are you ready to leave?" he asked.

She smiled. "Yes."

Chapter Two

Jensen drove, Nica in the front passenger seat, Tanner in the back.

The brothers kept up a steady conversation about nothing at all but an undercurrent of desire hummed between the three of them. It filled the air and her *arus* soaked it in like a sponge with water.

Magic rose through her body, making her flesh tingle and her sex clench. Blessed Goddess, the power she could channel with these two. Too bad they were *eteri* and could never know exactly what she was…

When Jensen parked halfway down a short side street a few blocks from Museum Road, she turned to see a white, two-story cottage that looked like something out of a fairy tale. And momentarily forgot how turned-on she was.

She turned to Jensen. "Is this yours?"

He shut off the car before looking first at her then past her to the house. "Yeah. We've still got some stuff to do to the exterior. New shutters, another coat of paint. We focused on the interior during the winter."

"It's still a little rough," Tanner added. "We don't have a lot of time to work on it during the summer."

"It's adorable."

Both men snorted identically as they pushed open their doors and stepped out of the high-riding SUV. Tanner immediately opened her door and helped her down to the sidewalk.

"Sweetheart, men's homes are not adorable." He continued to hold onto her hand as she stepped onto the sidewalk.

"Well, this one definitely is. I love it."

The house had two stories, the second slightly smaller than the first. Huge windows on both floors had dark shutters on either side and the roof was flat though it dipped down in front to almost touch the top of the second-story windows. None of the houses on the street remotely resembled each other and this one appealed to her like none of the others.

She couldn't wait to see the inside.

Jensen walked ahead to open the front door and wave her through. Tanner slid past her and turned left, flipping on a light and illuminating a sitting room as he continued into the kitchen at the back of the house.

"Do you want something to drink?" Tanner asked as he opened the fridge, grabbing a bottle of water.

Behind her, she heard Jensen close and lock the door.

And her breath caught in her throat, her stomach clenching in anticipation.

Jensen stopped next to her, drawing her gaze. He watched her with those blue eyes, the hunger and heat she saw there ensnaring her attention.

His hands, large and solid, cupped her face, the warmth of his skin sending shivers down her back, forcing her lips to part so she could breathe.

He held her gaze for so long, she thought she might have to kiss him. Vaguely, she heard the refrigerator door close then footsteps sounded on the wooden floor behind her.

Would Jensen kiss her first or would Tanner touch her?

Each second that passed as she waited for the answer tortured her.

When Jensen finally moved, she drew in a deep breath. And when his lips touched hers, her mind blanked to everything but the sensation of his skin on hers.

He moved his lips over hers slowly, as if savoring. Then his mouth opened over hers, his tongue slipping between her lips to stroke along hers.

Nica sank into the kiss, gave herself up to the waterfall of sensation it caused.

Jensen kissed with the same intensity he'd shown earlier in the bar. Totally focused on her, he overwhelmed her and she drowned in him. All while touching her nowhere but her face. And still, her entire body vibrated, hanging on the edge of expectation.

Her hands lifted to his hips, grasping at the waistband of his pants, though she didn't know if she needed an anchor or if she wanted to anchor him to her.

Her heart pounded against her ribs, her mouth and body responding eagerly to Jensen while waiting for Tanner's touch.

With her eyes closed, her other senses went on overload. Her ears strained for the slightest hint that Tanner was moving closer. She swore she felt his body heat on her back through the thin material of her shirt.

And still he didn't touch her.

Was he watching? Was that all he'd do?

Would it matter?

Tilting her head to the side, she started to give back to Jensen as good as she got. Opening her mouth just a little more, she slid her tongue along his, encouraging him to kiss her harder

With a groan that rumbled against her chest, Jensen's fingers slid across her cheeks and into her hair, shivers radiating out from the point of contact. His hands sank into her hair, the strands catching and pulling, erotic little tugs that made her moan.

Her hands clenched and pulled his hips closer. She needed to feel how much he wanted her, needed to know that he did.

And he didn't disappoint. His erection thick and hard against her lower stomach, she shifted, rubbing against him to ease the growing ache between her legs.

As if she'd given him permission, Jensen's hands released her hair and settled on her shoulders then slid down her arms, as if to warm her. His rough caress added fuel to the burn already boiling through her blood.

When he started to ease away from her mouth, she tried to maintain the contact as long as possible. She didn't want to stop, not for anything.

Finally Jensen pulled away, holding her in place. When she opened her eyes and stared into his, she saw fierce passion in every line of his expression.

She'd never seen that look on a man's face directed at her. It weighed down the air in the room, glazing it with sex and heat and promise.

A second pair of hands settled on her hips, and she drew in a rough breath, which turned into a shaky exhalation when Tanner pressed himself against her back and lowered his head to press his lips to her neck.

The experience was like nothing she'd had before. Better than the successful completion of her first spell or her first orgasm with a man.

Tanner's lips were softer than Jensen's but no less demanding, stringing kisses along the line of her neck until he reached her ear, which he bit. She shuddered, her lips parting, and both men recognized it as the symbol of surrender it was.

Though she refused to be a passive participant.

She reached for Jensen's tie as Tanner licked her earlobe into his mouth and sucked on it. Her fingers struggled to release the knot as she felt Tanner work her t-shirt from the waistband of her jeans and slide his hands against her bare skin.

"You have the softest skin," Tanner spoke into her ear, his warm breath causing her fingers to falter.

But Jensen wouldn't let her forget about him. He covered her hands with his and urged her to continue with his tie. It was something of a miracle she could get her fingers to cooperate because Tanner's hands had moved around her front and started to slide up her stomach to cup her breasts.

Wet heat coated her sex in a rush and she swore a tiny orgasm lit through her, just from Tanner's hands on her breasts.

And think how much better this will be when we're naked.

Her fingers found renewed purpose as she stripped Jensen's tie then started on his shirt buttons. His gaze remained riveted on hers and she worked by touch until she had the shirt unbuttoned.

Tanner's hands began to knead her breasts, and her focus faltered again, her fingers slowing. Jensen took matters into his own hands now and began to strip off his clothes. He didn't rush but he didn't do a slow striptease either. He moved with an economy of purpose that she recognized after spending only hours with him.

When he'd shed his shirt, her mouth dried at the sight of his toned upper body, his chest lightly covered with hair a shade darker than that on his head.

Her hands settled over his pecs, feeling the gentle prickle of that hair, fingers brushing across his flat brown nipples, teasing them into points as his breathing began to roughen.

"He likes that." Tanner nipped at her jaw, his hands still kneading her breasts with a slow, steady pressure. Her own nipples tightened and throbbed but he didn't touch them. In fact, he seemed to consciously avoid them. "He'll like it better if you put your mouth on them."

Heading the command in Tanner's voice, she leaned forward and settled her teeth around Jensen's nipple. When she bit down, Jensen's hands shot to her head to hold her there.

Her tongue swirled around the tight nub, licking away the slight hurt from her teeth. Jensen rewarded her with a tortured groan.

As she concentrated on Jensen once again, Tanner released her. She felt him move away and though she wanted more, she didn't want to leave Jensen.

Hearing movement behind her, she realized Tanner was stripping.

Lifting her head, she caught a quick glimpse of Jensen's burning gaze before he grabbed her and spun her to face Tanner. Shirtless, Tanner had his hands on his waistband, pushing his pants to the floor.

Dazed and so turned-on she could barely breathe, Nica watched Tanner shove his pants down his legs, taking his boxers with them and leaving him naked. Long and lean like a swimmer, he had a sleekly muscled chest and ripped abs. And his cock was a long, thick shaft that pulsed under her gaze.

She would have reached for him but Jensen grabbed the hem of her shirt and pulled it over her head. Her bra fell away next before he released the button on her jeans, drew down the zipper and shucked her pants along with her sandals.

Tanner's grin spread across his face, lighting a warmth deep inside, completely different from the desire. She'd never seen anyone so happy to see her naked. And that was a huge boost to her ego.

She smiled at him in return just before Jensen scooped her up into his arms. She gasped, her startled gaze rising to his face as he walked past the front door to a hallway that led through the house.

Following behind, Tanner flipped a switch on the wall and a soft glow from recessed lights in the ceiling lit the way.

A short hallway past a formal dining room and a large living room led straight to a bedroom shrouded in shadow. The light from the hallway penetrated far enough into the room for her to see the huge platform bed in the center.

And that was all she registered before Jensen sank onto the side of the mattress, muscles in his arms bulging as he lifted her above him. Her legs instinctively fell apart to straddle his thighs, her smooth skin tickled by the hair on his legs.

She smiled as her hands settled on his shoulders and Jensen's gaze drifted down her body before slowly moving back up.

"Now's the time to say no, Nica." Jenson's voice held a rough quality that stroked along her libido, sinking her deeper into desire.

She wanted to lean into him, rub her breasts against his chest but she forced herself to focus on those blue, blue eyes that promised so much pleasure. "I'm not going to say no. To either of you. Can't you tell how much I want this?"

She did want this. Wanted to be swept away, taken out of herself, to forget what her life was to become.

Tonight might be the only time they had and she wasn't going to waste it by being frightened.

"Then give yourself over to us." Tanner's hands settled on her shoulders, his voice low and smooth. "We'll take it from here."

Tanner's mouth settled onto the curve of her neck and shoulder at the same time Jensen's lips surrounded her nipple and drew her into the wet warmth of his mouth.

Nica closed her eyes and let her head drop back onto Tanner's chest, absorbing the sensations of their lips moving over her skin with a surety of purpose.

Her heart pounded out a hard and fast rhythm and her sex clenched with dizzying desire. As if he'd read her mind, Jensen's hand began a slow, steady caress of her leg, from her hip to her knee and back again. Each time he dragged his hand up her thigh, he got closer to her aching sex.

And each time, her breath caught and held until he moved it away again.

"Do you like that, sweetheart?" Tanner whispered in her ear, tightening every muscle in her body.

Gods, yes. She loved what they were doing to her. But she couldn't get her brain to form coherent sentences. She could only moan and turn her head to seek out a kiss.

She felt her sense begin to slip away and she had a sudden fear of what she might do if she lost control with these *eteri*. She couldn't reveal her powers, but what they made her feel was fast loosening her hold on her control.

She wanted to be swept away, to forget—

As if he felt her concentration slipping, Jensen's hand settled over her mound, his fingers sliding through her wet lower lips and setting off a small series of tremors.

"Please, yes." She could barely get the words out. "Touch me there."

"Oh we will, Nica. Both of us. That's what you want, right?"

"Yes, please. Both."

As abruptly as Jensen's hand had touched her, he drew away, causing her to cry out. But the men had no intention of abandoning her. Instead, she felt them moving, repositioning.

Tanner lifted her as Jensen slid back onto the bed. Then Tanner settled her against his brother, who immediately pulled her into his arms as they lay on their sides.

Jensen's cock lay hot and hard against her stomach as his mouth closed over hers. She thrust against him, her body moving on its own accord to get what it wanted.

"Slow down, baby. We've got all night."

Jensen's voice, so different from his brother's, made her open her eyes and stare into his. Even in the shadows of the bedroom, she thought she could see just how blue they were. Those eyes had been what attracted her to him in the first place. And now they anchored her in the moment.

"I don't want to slow down." She lifted her hands to cup his face. "Fast now, slow next time."

Jensen smiled, a flat-out grin that stole her breath. "I like the way you think."

With a speed that left her gasping, Jensen sat up and repositioned himself on his haunches farther down the bed. Turning onto her back, she had a second's glance of Jensen spreading her legs and moving between them before Tanner turned her head and kissed her.

This kiss was hungry, harder. Tanner pressed her head into the soft pillows, his erection rubbing against her hip. She could barely breathe, and when Jensen put his mouth over her sex, she cried out. Tanner swallowed the sound as his tongue fucked her mouth with the same rhythm Jensen licked at her clit.

Wicked, decadent pleasure coursed through her body and she became an elemental creature of sensation.

Jensen held her hips, pinning her lower body to the bed, while Tanner cupped her face in his hands. Her hands lifted to Tanner's shoulders, trying to draw him closer. He wouldn't budge, and, as Jensen pushed her closer to orgasm with his flickering tongue, Tanner slowed his kiss. She thought she might have to claw him to get him to give her what she wanted, which was faster and harder.

They'd done this before. They were good at it. And they expected her to lie back and let them take her.

But she wanted more.

She pushed Tanner away so she could look into his eyes. His expression showed his sudden fear that they'd pushed her too far.

Too turned-on to speak, she reached instead for Tanner's cock and tried to show him what she wanted. She pumped him with long, smooth strokes then wrapped her hands around the base and tugged.

Tanner's expression went sharp as he picked up on her signal. "I'm safe," he whispered. "We both are but let me get a condom."

She knew they were both physically safe. She'd seen no hint of disease in their auras.

"You don't need it. I'm clean and protected." And her magic would take care of any infection. "Come here, Tanner. I want to suck you."

If her hands had excited him, her words inflamed him. She swore she felt the temperature in the room rise by ten degrees and the energy tripled. Her *arus* slipped away from her tight control for the briefest second and both men groaned as that power reached out to them, wanting to siphon their energy.

Gods, what she wouldn't give to be able to let it loose. She knew from experience that power would make their orgasm amazing.

But these men were *eteri*. They wouldn't understand, would have questions she couldn't answer.

So with a concentrated effort, she dragged that power back under control, tucked it away.

And put her lips around Tanner's long, thick cock. She drew on his warm, hard flesh, swirling her tongue around the tip before taking him deeper.

Held on the tip of orgasm by Jensen's mouth, knowing she held Tanner on the edge of his own, Nica felt consumed. At the precipice.

And when her body broke with the scrape of Jensen's teeth across her clit, she made sure she took Tanner with her.

He came with a shout as her own climax continued to rack her body. Shaking with the power of it, her mouth still milking Tanner's pulsing cock, she barely noticed Jensen moving. But then another cock lodged at the entrance to her sex and Jensen thrust all the way to the hilt.

Her scream lodged in her chest as Jensen began to fuck her hard and fast.

Tanner pulled away, allowing her to cry out, but his mouth moved to her breasts, sucking first one then the other hard nub into his mouth.

Still sensitized by her first orgasm, she tipped into another one, this one making her back bow and her body shake as she tightened around Jensen's cock.

Jensen groaned, his hands tightening on her hips and his teeth lodging into the soft flesh of her neck as he came with a rough groan.

As she lay gasping, Tanner flopped onto the bed next to her and hugged her close, his arm just under her breasts.

After several seconds, she opened her eyes to find Jensen on his haunches, their bodies still connected. His gaze locked with hers as he slowly pulled out.

He'd sheathed himself with a condom. She hadn't even noticed. Faint disappointment fluttered through her, even though she understood his reasons.

She couldn't exactly tell them she'd checked them magically and found them disease-free, now could she?

Still…

His hand smoothed over her belly to run gentle fingers over her chin. Then he moved to the side and stood.

"I'll be right back."

She smiled, glanced at Tanner's arm pinning her to the bed. "I'm not going anywhere. Not yet."

"Damn straight." Tanner's muffled response made her smile widen and Jensen bent to kiss her. Hard. Hot.

"Do you want anything? Something to drink?"

She shook her head. "Just…hurry back."

She didn't want to waste a minute of their time tonight. She wanted more of both of them.

* * * *

Jensen headed to the kitchen for a bottle of water, stifling the urge to whistle like a fool.

He didn't whistle, not after mind-blowing sex. Typically, he fell asleep, pissing off his partner in the process, but Tanner was usually there to soothe any ruffled feathers.

Now he felt exhilarated. Hell, he felt happy. And he hadn't felt like this in a damn long time.

At the fridge, he pulled out a bottle of water and finished half of it in one gulp. He'd considered a shot of tequila but didn't want to dilute the natural high.

He knew Tanner felt the same.

Sure, some people considered them perverts or degenerates when they discovered they shared their women. Not that they went out and told the world how they lived their lives. Still, some women, after the first rush of excitement wore off, started to ask questions.

The most common—"Do you secretly want each other?"

That one always gave him the creeps.

Fuck, no, he didn't want to do his brother. That was just wrong on so many levels.

There was nothing perverted about his feelings for his brother. He loved Tanner but not in any fucked-up, sexual way.

All right, maybe they were perverted in the fact that he felt absolutely no jealousy with Tanner. And sure, watching his brother fuck a woman they both wanted made him hot. Just not for his brother.

Tanner always joked that psychologists would have a field day with them. Jensen never wanted to have anyone pick into his brain like that. Growing up, their lives had been a struggle, to say the least. But they'd come through. They'd stuck together. Hell, they actually liked each other, enough that they ran a business together and lived in the same house.

And no, they didn't share the same room.

Christ, people were sick.

He and Tanner just knew each other, knew their strengths and weaknesses. They knew what they liked, the type of woman who turned them on. Usually, it was the same woman. They worked so damn well as a team, some women actually begged them for more.

Of course, after a while, those women decided they weren't up to the hassle of dealing with two men in their life at the same time.

Most wanted to keep Tanner. He, on the other hand, was more of a project.

So what did Nica think?

As he gulped down the rest of the water, he realized it was the first time he'd thought about what their partner was thinking afterward.

There was something about Nica. She was different, on some level he hadn't quite figured out yet.

Grabbing two more water bottles from the fridge, he started to head back to the bedroom but heard a noise from the front room, something out of place.

A song, he realized. Coming from Nica's purse. Probably her phone.

A quick look at the clock on the fireplace mantel told him it was nearly three a.m. Who'd be calling her this late?

He grabbed her purse and headed back to the room.

Stopping in the doorway, he leaned against the frame. Nica and Tanner hadn't moved.

His brother's long body lay sprawled over half of the king-size bed, his eyes closed, head on the pillows facing Nica.

She lay on her back in the middle of the bed, one arm above her head, naked from the waist up. Her beautiful breasts quivered with each breath, her hair spread over her shoulders and chest like dark ribbons.

He knew how soft her hair was, how good her skin smelled.

She was gorgeous. Why had he ever thought differently?

As he stood there, watching her breathe, the ringing in her purse started again.

With a short indrawn breath, Nica opened her eyes just as he moved toward the bed. Hell, if she caught him standing there staring, she'd probably think he was being creepy.

"This is the second time it rang." He held out her purse. "Figured you want to check it."

She sat up, pushing her hair behind her shoulders. She didn't seem at all uncomfortable with his nudity or hers as she reached for her bag.

But her expression showed worry when she pulled the phone out and looked at the number.

She immediately slid it open. "Tira, what's up? Is something wrong?"

Jensen's gaze narrowed at the worry in Nica's tone and Tanner propped his head on one hand to listen.

"Are you sure?" Nica said. "They said my name?"

She paused, listening, and Jensen moved closer to the bed, resting his hands on the footboard.

"Yeah, I think you're right." She flashed a look at Jensen then at Tanner. "I'll be there as soon as I can."

She closed the phone. "I'm afraid I need to get home. Something's come up."

"At three in the morning?"

Jensen wanted to take the bite out of his words the second they left his mouth. Still, he couldn't help but wonder what the hell was going on at three in the morning that she needed to take care of.

Yes, he knew great sex didn't entitle him or Tanner to her secrets. He just didn't like that hint of fear in her voice. It made him want to pull her against him and tell her he'd take care of it for her.

"Is there a problem?" Tanner asked although he shoved off the bed and reached for his clothes. "Is there something we can do to help?"

Jensen shook his head as Tanner, once again, knew exactly what to say to put a smile on a woman's face. Nica flashed Tanner that smile as she slid out of bed, still not making any move to cover her beautiful body.

"No, it's nothing earth-shattering. Just…something Tira and I need to handle. I'm sorry to make you—"

"No sorry needed," Tanner cut in. "Let me get dressed and I'll give you a ride home."

As Nica came around the side of the bed, Jensen stepped in front of her. "There's a bathroom there." He pointed to the door along the wall. "I'll get your clothes for you."

Her smiled dimmed just the slightest bit but she nodded as she said thanks and headed for the bathroom.

Shaking his head over his uncharacteristic caveman impression, Jensen went back to the living room to gather their clothes. When he returned, she stepped from the bathroom.

Tanner was nowhere to be seen.

"I didn't mean to pry." He handed over her clothes. "You just seemed…worried."

Nodding, she took her clothes and started to shimmy into them. And Jensen had to turn away and slip back into his pants before she noticed his erection.

"I'm sure it's nothing. Just Tira being careful. But we've had some, uh, disturbing phone calls lately and she doesn't like staying alone."

She was lying. Jensen was a pretty good judge of people and she was lying about something.

Again, none of his business.

And no, he still didn't like the fact that she didn't want to tell him.

Damn, he was an idiot.

More so, because he was going to ride along with her and Tanner. Just to make sure she didn't need their help.

* * * * *

Tanner ran upstairs to get a pair of jeans and a sweatshirt and came back to find Jensen and Nica dressed and standing by the front door, waiting for him.

They stood silently, Nica fiddling with something in her purse while Jensen stared at her.

Jensen was worried and Tanner couldn't say he blamed him.

Tanner had picked up on the undertone of Jensen and Nica's conversation at the bar. She'd been looking for an escape tonight. That's why she'd been there.

Whether she'd been searching for sexual oblivion or not, she'd certainly been looking for something to take her mind off her troubles. And now it seemed trouble had found her.

Or was she having that post-sex stress some women had after fucking two brothers. Some were okay in the moment but once their brain started to kick in after an orgasm, guilt jumped in with both feet.

He really hoped Nica didn't feel guilty. Tanner didn't do guilt. Pleasure was good for the soul. Didn't matter where you got it as long as you didn't hurt anyone. Nica hadn't shown any signs of guilt but now, with her head bent over her purse, he had to wonder.

And maybe he was reading too much into the situation.

Tanner looked at Jensen again and caught his brother's eye. Jensen nodded. He wanted Tanner to find out what was going on because Tanner was good at getting women to talk. Jensen typically let Tanner do most of the talking because Jensen believed he sucked at it. Which Tanner always thought was a cop-out.

Still, Nica looked seriously worried, though she tried to hide it behind a smile when she looked up at him.

"You know, you don't have to run me home. I can call for a taxi."

Jensen was right. She was scared.

Tanner gave her his brightest smile. "No problem, sweetheart. We'll get going right now. You live in the city, right? Have you had much trouble there?"

She shook her head. "No, no trouble. Our neighborhood is pretty quiet most of the time."

Tanner opened the door and waved her through, Jensen close on her heels. Jensen took the lead to the car after Tanner locked the front door, Nica between them.

The warm night air seemed to dampen any and all sound but that probably had more to do with it being three a.m. Tanner heard no car noise, no noise of any kind. Their neighborhood rolled up its sidewalks by ten o'clock most nights so that wasn't unusual.

But the man who stepped from between two parked cars in front of the house next door… He made Tanner reach for Nica just as Jensen stepped in front of her, shielding her from view.

Why? Hell if Tanner knew. He only knew whatever this guy wanted, it wasn't good.

"Hello, Niccola. I hope you don't mind me showing up like this but you left me little choice."

Tanner felt Nica freeze behind him but she spoke without any hint of fear. "I thought I was clear the first time we spoke. I have no interest in working for you."

The man came closer and—holy hell, he was built like a brick shithouse. Muscled from shiny, shaved head to shit-kickers-clad toe. Someone sent to do someone else's dirty work.

"Jensen, take Nica back to the house." Tanner never took his gaze away from the behemoth who kept moving closer.

What the hell could a guy like this want with Nica? What could she be wrapped up in?

The man smiled a toothy grin as Jensen moved in front of Nica, stepping next to Tanner to form a wall in front of her.

"Oh look," he mocked. "Aren't the *eteri* cute? Do they think they can protect you?"

Eteri? What the hell were *eteri*? Some foreign slang?

"I don't know who you are or who you're working for," Nica said, "but I will not help you."

"Now, I don't think you want to make such a hasty decision. It took us a long time to track one of you down. My employer will make it worth your while. It'll be easier if you just come with me."

Tanner had had enough. "There's no way she's going anywhere with you so you can turn around and leave before this gets ugly."

The guy didn't even look at him or Jensen. He kept his attention squarely on Nica. Jensen tensed and Tanner knew he was getting ready to jump the guy. Tanner wouldn't be far behind.

Then Jensen jerked as if something had hit him and Nica shouted, "No!"

Out of the corner of his eye, Tanner saw Jensen fall, clutching his chest as if he'd been shot. Tanner shot forward, aiming to tackle the guy in front of him. The thug pointed his empty hand toward Jensen, as if he held a gun. Tanner hadn't seen a shot or smelled gunpowder. All he knew was that his brother was down and this guy was responsible.

"Tanner, no!"

Nica's voice rang loud in the silence, a command in her tone he didn't heed.

He didn't get far before he was tossed backward.

He stumbled back into Jensen and Nica, who'd gone to her knees next to Jensen and gathered him into her arms. Tanner didn't have time to check on either of them because the guy still stood there. Not moving in for the kill. Just standing there staring at them.

No, not them. He was fixated on Nica.

"This is just a warning, Niccola. You have until Monday. Next time you will come willingly. Or there'll be more casualties."

Then the guy turned and walked away.

Tanner struggled to get to his feet but the guy must have hit him harder than he'd thought and he fell back on his ass on the pavement. His ears rang and his lungs felt as if someone had dropped a concrete block on them.

"Jensen, can you hear me? Jensen!"

The increasing panic in Nica's voice finally broke through Tanner's confusion and he turned to find Jensen out cold in Nica's arms.

Tanner scrambled to his knees, reaching to touch his brother's pale face. He didn't see any blood but... "Shit! Is he shot? Nica, what the hell happ—"

"We need to get him inside." She stared straight into his eyes, hers wide but not terrified. "You need to carry him inside and let me work on him. I can help him. You have to trust me."

Trust her to do what? Tanner struggled to his feet but could barely stand, the throbbing in his head made him dizzy. "Gotta get Jensen to the hospital." He reached for his cell phone to call 9-1-1 but it wasn't in his pocket.

"They won't be able to help him there." Nica's voice held a thread of strength, of command that made him want to listen to her. "You need to help me get him inside."

Yeah, okay. They needed to get inside. Tanner shut his mouth and reached for Jensen. His brother was shorter but carried more muscle weight than Tanner.

With his head still fuzzy and his knees weak, Tanner wasn't sure he could make it all the way into the house without dropping his brother, but between him and Nica, they got Jensen off the ground. They wrapped his arms around their shoulders and dragged his dead weight back into the house, laying Jensen out on the floor of the living room.

"Tanner, I need you to bring me a bowl of cold water, tap is fine. I'll need towels too. Go."

He went but not before he watched Nica tear open Jensen's shirt and lay her hands on his brother's unbroken skin. He saw no blood, no sign of a blow of any kind.

What the hell had that thug done? Tanner shook his head, trying to remember.

"Tanner." Nica didn't even bother to turn around. "Please, I need those things."

He went, got a bowl, filled it with ice then water. From the pantry, he grabbed the beach towels they stored there. Why the hell did they keep the beach towels in the pantry? What—

Shaking his head, he cleared his wandering thoughts and headed back to the living room.

Christ, if anything happened to Jensen—

"Holy fuck, what the hell?"

Tanner froze at the sight of Nica kneeling next to his brother, her hands flat on Jensen's chest. And glowing. Her hands actually glowed, a pale greenish yellow that pulsed as it bathed Jensen's chest in light.

"Put the water and towels next to me and step back but don't go anywhere," she said. "I may need your help."

"What the hell are you doing?"

"I'm drawing out the spell."

He did as she said, trying to think through the ache in his head. Did she just say spell?

"Did you call—"

"Tanner." Her quiet but forceful tone shut him up immediately. "I need to concentrate. Please."

She needed to concentrate. On drawing out the spell.

Christ, this was not happening.

Jensen was not lying on the floor, looking like he was dying. And Nica was not hunched over him, her hands glowing—freaking *glowing*—like something out of a sci-fi film.

He had to be dreaming.

That was the only explanation for the fact that he stood there and watched a woman he'd only known for a few hours move her glowing hands over his possibly dying brother.

Nica didn't make a sound as she concentrated, eyes closed, mouth moving in a silent rhythm. As if she were praying.

Tanner didn't have much religion. He believed in being a good person, doing the right thing and having fun without hurting anyone.

He didn't believe in faith healers. He didn't believe in magic.

But he couldn't dismiss what he saw with his own eyes. So that meant he had to be dreaming.

Nica gasped at that moment, her hands trembling and her body convulsing with a shudder.

"Gods damn it. That bastard."

He barely heard Nica mutter under breath but he knew she wasn't pleased.

"Tanner, come sit behind me. I need you."

Yeah, sure. Why not? This dream couldn't get any freakier.

He sat.

"Now, I know this is going to sound really strange..." She paused as she drew her hands away from Jensen and turned so she could look at him. "I need you to kiss me. I need energy to counteract the spell and sexual energy is the best way to do that."

She stared into his eyes, hers intense with concentration. She had beautiful eyes, a beautiful mouth. She had such a serene presence that the heat the three of them had generated in bed had been a surprise. A great one.

"I know you're worried about Jensen but I can help him," she continued. "I just need you to help me."

"Sure."

So he cupped her cheeks in his hands and kissed her. That's what you did in a dream. You went with it.

And kissing Nica was the best dream ever. Her soft lips felt like silk against his, her warm breath enticing him to fall a little deeper into her. He remembered how her mouth had felt wrapped around his cock, how she'd cried out around him when she'd come.

Now she melted against him, opened her mouth and kissed him back.

And he felt...something. Like a breeze from an open window blew over his skin. But they'd turned on the central air last week and all the windows in the house were closed.

It's a dream, only a dream.

A dream that felt way too real.

He snapped back, his eyes opening wide as that breeze lifted the hair on his arms. Static electricity.

Nica must have felt it too because she drew in a deep breath, her eyes still closed. As if she were basking in the feeling.

"Nica, what—"

She pressed her mouth to his again in a short, sharp kiss before she turned back to Jensen and replaced her hands on his brother's chest.

"Put your arms around me, Tanner. Hold me."

Sliding his arms around her waist, his hands splayed across her abdomen. She leaned into him without taking her hands away from Jensen. He felt every breath shudder through her body. And felt a warm energy that seemed to surround her like a haze.

What the hell…

Her hands began to glow again.

Jesus Christ, this was no dream.

His lungs caught on an indrawn breath then began to work on overload. "Nica, what the fuck is going on?"

She didn't answer right away, her concentration completely focused on his brother. As he watched over her shoulder, fear for his brother's life and sheer wonder at what Nica was doing combining to make him lightheaded.

The glow pulsed, as if in time with her heartbeat. He couldn't look away.

She began to chant again, this time audibly. He didn't recognize the language. Not French, which he'd taken in high school. Not Spanish, which some of their employees spoke.

Nica gasped, her expression pinching with pain, but her hands remained steady over Jensen. The glow changed color, flaring almost white before becoming so bright it hurt Tanner's eyes.

Then, like the flash of an explosion, the glow intensified so much, he had to close his eyes. Nica fell back against him as if someone had pushed her and he instinctively held her tighter.

When he opened his eyes, he looked first at Jensen and found his brother's eyes opening.

"Jesus, Tanner. What the hell happened?" Jensen sat up, shaking his head, as if shaking off a headache. "Shit. Nica, are you okay?"

Tanner looked down into Nica's pale face, slack in unconsciousness. Then he looked back at Jensen, who looked perfectly healthy.

"What the hell's going on?"

Tanner didn't realize he'd said the words aloud until Jensen answered him as he rose to his feet and lifted Nica out of his arms.

"I have no idea." Jensen carried her to the couch and set her down. "What the fuck happened?"

"Nothing happened," Nica said, her voice faint as she struggled to sit up on the couch. "Everything's fine."

Tanner snorted. "Yeah, well, that's bullshit."

His tone was harsher than he wanted and when she flinched, Jensen shot him a look. Tanner tried to tone down his anxiety but something weird was definitely going on. Nica was in trouble with a guy who'd laid out Jensen with a... Hell, he still didn't know how the guy had hit Jensen hard enough to knock him unconscious. And he'd seen Nica's hands glow. They'd fucking glowed and she'd held them over Jensen's body until he'd woken.

"Nica, who was that guy and what did he want with you? What did he do to Jensen? And what's with the glowing hands?"

His brother jerked around to look at him like he was nuts but Tanner knew what he'd seen. And when Nica didn't bother to contradict him, Jensen turned to her.

"What's he talking about?"

Nica shook her head. "I can't explain. You won't understand. And after the next few minutes, you won't remember."

Nica struggled up to sit on the couch.

Her head hurt from the force of the binding spell breaking. Her nerve endings tingled with residual energy and her hands burned.

"Could I please have the bowl? I need to soak my hand." The shock of the cool water would help until she got home and put her mother's salve on them.

That spell had been nasty and if she hadn't been as skilled as she was, Jensen would have died. It had bound all of his internal organs and forced them to stop. It would have killed him. Whoever the man was who'd worked it, he had power of his own, though the workings were a little crude. Effective but crude.

So who was he?

She thought about that as Jensen and Tanner continued to fire questions at her.

Questions she couldn't answer because they would never believe her. And if they did…well, that opened a whole other can of worms.

"Nica, you're in trouble. Let us help."

The intensity in Jensen's voice cut through the clamor in her head and she looked up at him. He held the bowl and she felt the couch dip as Tanner sat beside her, guiding her hands into the water. She breathed a sigh of relief as they cooled.

Yes, she was in trouble but they couldn't help.

Both men stared at her with the same level of concern, though Tanner's was tinged with a whole lot more "What the fuck?"

He'd seen her hands.

She stared straight into his eyes and lied, hating herself as she did it.

"Nothing happened. I don't know what you're talking about."

And when she was safe at home, and these men didn't remember a second of this night, then she could cry her heart out.

Because this was all her fault.

The calls had started a week ago. A female voice she didn't recognize had called the apartment, asked for her by name. The woman had said she wanted Nica to work for her, wanted her to use her "special gift" for her. She'd promised huge sums of cash.

At first, Nica had shrugged it off as a telemarketer. But the woman had called every day. Except today.

She shouldn't have gone to the bar tonight. She shouldn't have gone home with these *eteri*.

But, oh Blessed Goddess, they'd had been the best thing to happen in her life in more years than she cared to admit. They'd made her feel wanted for herself and not just her abilities. They'd made her feel sexy—

"Nica." Tanner's sharp tone cut through her thoughts. "Who was that guy?"

She shook her head. "I have no idea. I've never seen him before."

She answered truthfully, more because she still needed a few more minutes to recover. She had to perform the spell that would wipe the brothers' memories of this night but she wasn't as adept at this as Tira, whose Goddess Gift tied directly into her mental capabilities.

Nica's Gift drew from her emotions and right now, they were in upheaval. She wasn't sure she could remember the spell much less perform it correctly. Even though she knew she had to.

She couldn't leave without wiping their memories. They couldn't remember what had happened.

As the men continued to fire questions at her, she began the spell that would wipe her from their memories as surely as if they'd never met. Using the water as a conductor, she let the spell sink into the bowl. All her many years of training came to the fore as she charged the water.

"Nica!" Jensen's raised voice drew her gaze as she finished the spell.

"I'm sorry."

She cupped the water in her hand and flung a handful first at Tanner then at Jensen.

The absolute shock on their faces made her hold her breath. If the spell didn't work, they'd think she was crazy, call her a cab and put out a restraining order on a woman who didn't exist in their world.

"What the—" Tanner started but never finished and Nica knew the spell had taken hold.

Tears welled as Tanner's then Jensen's eyes lost focus. They stared into space as the spell reordered their memories, remade their image of her. They'd remember her tomorrow as a redhead, her features completely different. They'd think she'd left the bar with them but that they'd parted at the curb. She'd gone home, they'd gone home and no one had had mind-blowing sex.

They wouldn't remember her or the way they'd loved her. She'd become a ghost. Hell, she wouldn't even be a memory. She'd be nothing.

Not fair. So not fair.

Pulling her phone out of her pocket, she took a deep breath then dialed a number she'd committed to heart but hadn't needed to use. Until now.

After a brief conversation, she hung up and watched the best night of her life disappear before her eyes.

Chapter Three

Jensen woke up on the couch in the living room, his head pounding.

How the hell much did he drink last night?

He looked around and saw Tanner asleep on the recliner in the corner.

Damn, what the hell had they done?

Rubbing a hand over his face, he sat up, running his fingers through his hair and unbuttoning his shirt. He paused when he realized he was missing a button.

When had he lost that?

He remembered going to the bar last night, remembered he and Tanner talking to a woman, a redhead. Which was unusual because neither of them typically went for redheads.

They'd walked out of the bar together but they'd parted company at the curb and he and Tanner had come home alone.

Or had she come home with them?

No, if she'd come home, they wouldn't be sleeping here.

Goddamn, he knew he hadn't drunk that much.

He tossed a throw pillow at Tanner, who barely moved when it hit him.

"Tanner, wake the hell up."

"Fuck off, Jen." Tanner didn't even open his eyes, just grabbed the pillow and stuffed it under his head. "I'm sleeping."

"Tanner, come on. What'd we do last night?"

Bits and pieces of memories floated through his head but it didn't seem to make any sense. Like disjointed pieces of a picture that didn't quite add up to a whole.

And he remembered having the weirdest fucking dream…about a woman who'd vanished in midair. From right there. In the middle of the living room.

She needs help. You shouldn't have let her go.

"Tanner, get the hell up. Something happened. Something's…wrong."

But what? Why the hell did he think something was wrong?

Tanner opened his eyes enough to squint at him. "What are you…" He shook his head and sat up, his expression evolving from sleepy disorientation to confusion. Looking down at his clothes then around at the room, he finally lifted his gaze back to Jensen's.

"We went to that bar last night, the one Daniel told us about," Tanner said. "We talked to a woman, a redhead. Then we came home. Alone."

Jensen shook his head. "Yeah, that's what I remember too. But…I had a weird dream last night. About a woman who—"

"Disappeared right there." Tanner pointed at the middle of the room. "I had the same dream."

"We haven't done that since we were kids."

Tanner nodded, his expression tightening. "What'd she look like?"

"Dark hair, dark eyes. Pretty. Quiet."

"Serene."

Yeah, that was the perfect word. "Who was she?"

"I don't have a fucking clue," Tanner practically growled. "But she's in trouble."

"I know. How do we know that?"

"Again, I have no clue. I just… Jesus, this is like an episode of *Supernatural*."

Jensen didn't laugh at the joke like he normally did. Whenever something vaguely weird happened, whether a light bulb blew or their keys turned up somewhere they didn't belong, Tanner would make some crack about the TV show with two brothers who fought supernatural villains. That Jensen's name was the same as one of the show's stars just made Tanner work that much harder to crack those jokes.

Right now, it wasn't funny. Because something really weird was going on.

"We need to find her." Jensen knew that for an absolute fact. She needed them. And he wanted her back. Now.

Tanner was shaking his head. "This is really weird."

"I know. We need to go back to the bar. We met her at the bar, right?"

Or had they?

Tanner sighed, his gaze searching the floor as if for answers. "I only remember the redhead. Did you try to pick her up?"

Jensen shook his head. "You know I don't go for redheads. And neither do you."

Tanner sighed. "We need to go back to that bar."

* * * * *

"Are you sure you're going to be okay here alone? I can stay—"

"Sal, really. I'm fine."

Well, she wasn't but she wasn't about to tell the legendary *salbinelli* Salvatorus, powerful guardian of the Etruscan race, that all she wanted was for him to leave so she could curl up in a ball and cry in peace.

Sal clomped over to her, the sound of his hooves muffled by the carpet on the living room floor of the safe house he ran for the Etruscans.

Inches shorter than her own five-two, Sal had handsome Etruscan features, glossy black curls and tiny black horns peeking out of those curls. Muscles packed his upper body—his shoulders, his arms, his broad chest—until his lower stomach. Where what had been human became goat.

She wondered what Tanner and Jensen would do if they ever got a look at Sal. Would they run screaming?

No, they wouldn't run. They hadn't run last night. They'd stepped in front of her to protect her.

Would they try to hurt Sal? Attack him for being different?

She'd seen Tanner's expression as he watched her hands. He'd been dumbfounded. But not disgusted.

Of course, he'd been too stunned to completely understand what was going on. And he'd been terrified for his brother's life.

But even then, he'd trusted her enough to let her unbind the spell that had been shutting down Jensen's internal organs.

"Niccola, I don't think I should leave you alone." Sal sat on the couch next to her and put his hand on her shoulder. "Babe, I don't figure you want me to call your mom but—"

"Goddess no." She shuddered. "I'm no longer a child. And my life will be over soon enough."

Damn it, she hadn't meant to say that aloud.

Closing her eyes, she wished the words would magically disappear. Sal probably thought she was an ungrateful bitch.

He didn't know her well. They'd only met once or twice when he'd been to her tiny village to see one of the *streghe* about something. He led a secluded life because of the nature of who and what he was. He could go out on the street in the guise of a young boy if he worked a powerful enough glamour. But the magic needed to hold the illusion for any length of time required a huge expenditure of power.

Power was something Sal was said to have an almost unending supply of but he used it in his position as guardian for the Etruscans. He shielded this safe house, which hadn't been discovered in the two hundred years since he'd opened it. And he got foolish women out of messes like the one she'd gotten into last night.

She'd been given a powerful Goddess Gift to serve her people and all she'd done was complain about it for the past several months. And now someone knew who she was and what she could do.

Total bitch.

"I'm sorry, Sal." She sighed. "I am not ungrateful. Just…"

"Feeling a little trapped?"

Her gaze flew up from her dissection of her shoes to meet his gaze. "I… No, not trapped, just… Tinia's teat, yes, I'm feeling trapped. And it really doesn't make me feel any better to actually say that. It just makes me feel worse."

"Okay then," Sal said. "Here's something to do while you sit here and mope. I've got a computer in the next room. There's a file on it with pictures of known *Malandante* enforcers. It's right on the desktop called *Mal*. Yeah, I know. Original. Go through the pictures. See if you recognize the guy who attacked you while I'm gone."

"Do you think he'll go after Tira? Or Jensen and Tanner?"

"Tira should be fine. Her foresight will act as an early warning system and she's agreed to lay low for the next day or so until we figure out what's going on and who this guy is."

Sal paused and she forced herself to meet his dark solemn eyes.

Maybe she didn't want to hear the answer to her question.

"I think, if whoever's after you thinks he can draw you out by going after the Miller brothers, he will. Short of breaking all kinds of written and unwritten rules about *eteri* knowing about Etruscans, they're on their own."

Her heart twisted but she'd known what he was going to say.

She never should have gone home with them last night. And she'd never see them again.

And if something happened to them, she'd blame herself for the rest of her life.

* * * * *

Jensen walked into Lacey's Stay-A-While and stopped just inside the door.

He let his gaze travel over the entire room, stopping to thoroughly examine every woman in the place.

Which didn't take long. It was still early for a Saturday, only around six, but he hadn't wanted to wait at the house any longer. Tanner had a meeting he couldn't miss but he'd be there as soon as that ended. Hopefully by then, Jensen would've found the woman.

His unease had grown all day and he hated the sense of disorientation that came with it. Like someone had gone into his brain and scrambled his memories. Why someone would do that or even how someone would do that made it all the more ludicrous.

And yet...

Walking up to the bar, he sat at a stool at the far end, away from the door so he'd have a clear view of anyone entering or leaving.

The male bartender he remembered from last night walked over. He didn't see the female owner, Lacey.

"What can I get you?"

His stomach rumbled at the smell of grilling meat and tomato sauce wafting around the room. "A menu? Food smells great."

The bartender laid one on the counter, still eyeing him. "You were in last night. You just move to the area?"

Jensen flashed the guy a look, noting the shoulder-length brown hair, the intent hazel eyes and the hard expression. As if he knew Jensen had questions. But that was stupid. Why would this guy think Jensen was there for anything other than dinner and a few drinks? Paranoia must be gaining on him.

"Born and raised in Robesonia," Jensen finally answered. "Nice place."

"Yeah, my wife thinks so. It's hers. I'm Teodoro de Feo."

Okay, maybe that explained the guy's interest in him. He was warning Jensen away from his wife. Maybe he'd be happy to hear Jensen was looking for another woman.

"Jensen Miller." He stuck out his hand, which de Feo took without hesitation. "Nice to meet you."

The other man nodded even as he acknowledged the two guys who'd just sat at the end of the bar. "I'll be back in a minute to take your order."

After figuring out what he wanted, Jensen waited for Teodoro—What was that? Italian?—to return, wondering how he should go about asking what was probably going to sound like an idiotic question.

Hey buddy, could you describe the woman I was with last night? Was she a redhead or a brunette? Did my brother and I leave with her? And can you tell me where she lives because I think she's in trouble? Why? Hell if I know.

Yeah, that'd go over real well.

"So, what'll ya have?" Teodoro stood in front of him, watching him with sharp eyes.

Jensen ordered a burger and fries and a beer, which Teodoro tapped and set in front of him after putting in his food order.

"You look like a man with a question, Jensen Miller. Wanna tell me what it is?"

Jensen set his beer back on the bar and looked the guy straight in the eyes. "The woman I was with last night. Do you know who she is?"

Teodoro crossed his arms over his chest, never taking his eyes off Jensen. "Never saw her before."

"But you did see me with a woman last night."

His eyes narrowing, Teodoro nodded. "Yeah, a redhe—"

"No. Not a redhead." Jensen shook his head. "The brunette."

Teodoro froze for a millisecond and if Jensen hadn't been watching so closely, he never would've noticed it. But the guy definitely knew something about his mystery woman. "Didn't notice the brunette. Sorry. Food'll be out in a few minutes."

Then Teodoro moved down the bar and out onto the floor to take orders from a table along the wall.

Bullshit.

The guy had lied straight to his face without a tell. Too bad for him that Jensen could read people. And Teodoro de Feo was lying.

But why?

* * * * *

"Are you sure it's him?"

Teo's snort sounded like a whip crack through the phone line. "Positive. It's Jensen Miller. Introduced himself then started asking questions about the woman he was with last night. Good thing Sal called to warn us this morning or I would've spilled.

"I had Rio do background checks. No records, neither of them have so much as a speeding ticket. Good business reputations, well respected in the community. Sounds like they had a pretty gods-awful childhood, though. Dad was a mean drunk, apparently. Their mom killed him in self-defense when they were twelve. They saw it all.

"Their mom wasn't quite right after that and they took care of her until she died when they were nineteen. Put themselves through college and used the money their old man left to start their construction business."

Blessed Goddess, not fair. So not fair.

She'd known when she met them that they were not just average guys out to have a good time and get laid. They'd lived through hell and become better men for it. Men she'd never see again.

"Nica." Teo voice shocked her through the line. "You want me to get rid of him?"

Nica sighed, her chest tightening with fear. Not for herself though. For Jensen and Tanner.

She must have screwed up the spell somehow. They remembered her.

And if the man who'd come after her last night decided the Miller brothers knew something about her, he didn't seem like the kind of guy who'd use a lot of restraint when it came to questioning *eteri*.

Now what?

"Nica? Still there?"

"Yes, I'm still here. I just...don't know what to do. Sal's not back yet but I don't like not telling the guys they might be in danger. If anything happens to them..."

It would be her fault. Because she'd indulged herself when she had no business doing so.

"Cam's still trying to track the guy from last night." Teo, his older brother, Cam, and their two other brothers ran a supernatural security agency. As *linchetto*, night elves, they had special abilities that made their choice of profession a natural fit. "He's not coming up with anything. Even though you weren't able to identify him as *Mal* doesn't mean he isn't. Just stay put, Nica."

She hung up after saying goodbye but she couldn't stay still. She paced, not able to sit and watch TV as she waited for either Sal or Cam de Feo to call.

Waiting sucked. She felt like she'd been waiting all her life. Waiting for her mother to step down, waiting for her life to begin.

She was really sick and tired of waiting.

Her mother was always telling her how powerful she was, how she would be an asset to her people.

Well, this asset was not about to let two innocent men be harmed because of her. She would go to them, get them to invite her back to their house. If the man from the other night attacked again, she'd be there to defend the brothers. Or at least try.

And she'd get to spend another amazing night with the two men who'd rocked her world.

Grabbing her purse, she headed for the door. She wouldn't think about what she'd do if they didn't ask her to go home with them. They remembered enough about her to go back to the bar and ask for her. They must want to see her again.

Her heart tripped over itself at the thought. And if she could keep them sufficiently occupied, maybe they'd ask her to stay until Monday.

The man who'd attacked them had said he'd be in touch Monday. By then the de Feos should know who the guy was, what he wanted and who he was working for.

She hoped.

And before she left the Miller brothers, she'd wipe their memories again. She'd do it right this time.

They'd be safe. And ignorant of the magic in the world.

She'd have the rest of her life to regret leaving them. But hopefully she'd have wonderful memories to sustain her.

* * * * *

Tanner walked into the bar, ready for a beer and for Jensen to tell him he'd found the woman.

He hadn't been in touch with his brother because his cell phone had died. He'd forgotten to plug it in last night.

Another anomaly. He never forgot to plug in his phone.

He found his brother sitting at a table, finishing off a burger and fries. His stomach rumbled.

Jensen looked up as he sat down. "Food's good."

Okay, maybe he'd eat. But first, "What'd you find?"

Jensen swallowed, wiped his mouth with a napkin and settled back in his chair. His gaze slid to the bar for a brief second before he met Tanner's gaze again.

"We're not crazy."

"She was here." Tanner didn't make it a question and his chest tightened with excitement. Which didn't make a damn bit of sense. They still had so many unanswered questions.

Yeah, but she's real. And we can see her again.

Jensen nodded as if he'd read his mind. "The bartender tried to bullshit me but he knew who I was talking about. I figure he already called to let her know we're here."

Would she avoid them like the plague? And why the hell were both of their memories of last night more like dreams?

Had she slipped them a drug? But why? It didn't make any sense unless she hadn't wanted them to remember her. Again, why?

"So now what?"

Sighing, Jensen shook his head. "Tell the bartender we think she's in trouble but don't know why? And that we don't even know her name? Tell him we both had the same dream about her? Which of these don't make us look like complete psychos?"

"Do you think she drugged us?" Even as he said it aloud, Tanner knew it hadn't been a drug. He knew what drugs did to the body. Their father had used them often enough on him and Jensen when they were kids that they both knew the effects.

Jensen shook his head even as he said, "That'd seem to be the only rational explanation."

Maybe rational wasn't going to cut it for this situation. "Maybe we need to look for irrational explanations."

"Then we need to get him to talk."

They both turned to look at the bartender, standing behind the bar, staring at them.

He wasn't glaring, wasn't scowling. His expression showed absolutely nothing of his thoughts. Until his gaze shifted and his eyes narrowed. He set down the glass he'd just picked up and walked to the end of the bar.

Tanner turned to look at the front door.

And found himself staring straight into the eyes of their dream woman.

* * * * *

Jensen stood, almost knocking over the chair in his haste as he took several steps toward the door before stopping.

Shit. He didn't want to scare her by rushing at her like a crazed bull. He didn't want her to run.

Not that she looked scared. No, she looked…determined. She must have known they were here because she didn't seem surprised to see them. He figured the bartender had called to warn her.

And she'd still shown up. Did that mean she wanted to see them again?

Was he nuts to be happy about that, considering he didn't have a clue what had really happened last night?

Hell, he didn't even remember her name. But when he looked at her, heat burned low in his gut before flooding through his blood. He wanted her. Hell, he had a hard-on already just staring at her.

His fingers itched to run through that long hair, and he knew it would feel like silk. He knew because he'd had his fingers in it.

Goddamn, what the hell had happened last night?

Behind him, he heard Tanner stand as well.

Her expressive face flashed her every emotion—distress, confusion and a healthy dose of desire.

Then she tilted her chin up and started to wind her way through the tables to them. She flashed a look at the bar and Jensen saw her hold off the bartender with one shake of her head.

The guy looked ready to jump the bar and come to her aid, as if he and Tanner were dangerous. That, more than anything, made Jensen take a deep breath and a step back.

He didn't want her to be frightened of them. He just wanted answers.

And he wanted her.

She didn't smile as she got closer, didn't try to hide the fact that she was nervous. About talking to them? Why?

When she reached them, she stopped only inches away from Jensen, as if she didn't want anyone else to hear her. The bar wasn't crowded but a few of the tables close to them were taken. No one seemed to be paying any attention to them, though.

She tried out a smile but it didn't quite seem natural. "Hello again, Jensen. Tanner."

Jensen's gaze narrowed at her use of "again". She admitted they'd met.

Tanner stepped forward when Jensen didn't say anything.

"You have us at a disadvantage." Tanner held out his hand. "Your name is?"

Her smile faltered and panic flashed through her eyes for a brief second before she blinked it away. "Niccola Donato."

"Well, it's nice to meet you, Niccola." Tanner waved at the table, an easy smile on his face. "Why don't you sit down and let us buy you a drink."

"And then," Jensen crossed his arms over his chest, "you can tell us why we had the exact same dream about you."

Jensen practically heard Tanner's inward groan but he didn't want to beat around the bush.

Every second counted. He had no idea why he couldn't get the feeling that every second they stood here exchanging meaningless bullshit, someone was getting closer to her. Someone who wanted to hurt her.

Niccola flushed as she sat. "I don't know. We talked for much of the night. I very much enjoyed the time we spent together. I asked Teo to call me if you showed up tonight. I hope you don't mind. I really wanted to see you again."

Jensen opened his mouth ask her why the hell they'd both dreamed about her last night but Tanner kicked him in the shin and cut in.

"Well, we're definitely glad to see you again. Jensen, why don't you order drinks?"

"I don't want a drink." She looked at Tanner then turned to Jensen, and her gaze practically burned his skin. "I want to take you up on your invitation from last night. I'd like to go home with you."

Chapter Four

Nica stepped inside the guys' adorable house after Jensen, her heart pounding, her pussy already wet and aching for them.

The brothers had hustled her out of the bar seconds after she'd dropped her bombshell.

They hadn't looked surprised. They'd just flashed each other a look then waved her out the door, straight to their car. They didn't even ask if she had a car, which she didn't. She'd taken a cab from Sal's.

Now she wondered if they'd grill her, if they'd ask questions she had no answers to.

She forced herself to stop in the entry as Jensen walked ahead into the small living room to the left of the door, where he turned on a table light.

Tanner pushed the front door shut behind him, the sound of the deadbolt clicking into place deafening in the silence.

Nica stopped in the foyer, attacked by a sudden case of nerves. What if, by going home with them again, she'd drawn the man from the other night back to them? He'd said he'd return for her answer Monday. Why not just wait at Sal's until Monday, wait for the man to approach her again with the de Feo brothers waiting to capture the man?

Had she selfishly put the Miller brothers' lives in more jeopardy simply by trying to keep them safe? And what happened if the spell she'd put on their memories broke by seeing her here, at the exact spot where she'd disappeared last night? She still wasn't exactly sure how she'd screwed up the spell last night. Maybe she hadn't really wanted them to forget her.

Hell, there was no maybe about that.

But—

No. She was here now and here she'd stay. Until they kicked her out or Monday arrived.

"Nica, are you—"

"I brought my medical record with me, if you want to see it," she blurted out, cutting off Tanner before he could finish his question. "I'm safe. And I want you to know…I don't normally do this."

She pulled the sheet of paper she made on the computer from her purse. She wanted the men to feel safe with her. That there was no need for a condom. She wanted nothing to get in their way tonight.

She caught and held Tanner's gaze, saw his gaze slide to his brother. Saw him nod at Jensen.

Tanner stepped forward as she held out the paper to him. He took it though he didn't look at it right away. Instead he stared down into her eyes, searching for something.

"Thank you."

His blue eyes were a little lighter than Jensen's though no less beautiful. She smiled straight into them and watched them fill with heat.

Behind her, she felt Jensen approach and turned to see him hold out two sheets of paper. He was silent, but his eyes burned.

Gods, she wanted to throw herself at them right now, make them satisfy the ache in her pussy, the desire.

Instead, she forced herself to take the papers, to read them, even though she knew they were fine.

When she finished, she held them out to Jensen who took them and let them fall to the floor, forgotten as he continued to stare at her.

When Tanner's hands curved around her hips from behind, she gasped, her gaze still glued to Jensen's.

She felt almost as if last night was repeating itself if it wasn't for the fact that Jensen didn't touch her. Instead, he watched Tanner's hands flatten on her stomach and draw her back against his body, pressing his rigid erection into the small of her back.

She wanted to close her eyes, to absorb the sensation but Jensen wouldn't release her gaze. He watched as Tanner's hands moved to cup her breasts, kneading them with firm pressure.

Her head fell back on Tanner's shoulder and she turned to kiss his stubbled jaw.

Closing her eyes as Tanner's mouth closed over hers, she cleared her mind of everything but the scent of his skin, the pressure of his hands on her and the weight of Jensen's gaze as he watched them.

Jensen had been the one to initiate their play last night. She wondered if, subconsciously, the brothers took turns going first. The thought elicited a smile that Tanner must have felt.

He pulled back to look at her, an answering grin on his lips. "We haven't even gotten to the really good stuff yet and you're already smiling. I hope that bodes well."

"I'm sure—" She gasped as Jensen picked that moment to cup her chin, turn her and drop his mouth over hers.

Oh Goddess, his kiss. She remembered from last night how forceful Jensen kissed and how it made every muscle in her body tighten in lust.

Except tonight, he acted as if he knew exactly what she wanted.

He kissed her until she actually felt her knees go weak. Tanner held her against him, steadied her as Jensen continued his onslaught.

She let him overwhelm her, let Tanner hold her up. She soaked in their heat, soaked in their energy. And felt herself give up all conscious thought. All she felt was sensation.

Jensen's mouth as he ravaged hers, Tanner's hands kneading her breasts. Jensen's hands on her hips then at the waistband of her jeans, unbuttoning, unzipping, pushing them down, taking her underwear with them.

When Jensen released her mouth, Tanner took the opportunity to lift her shirt over her head then removed her bra. She was naked and at their mercy in seconds.

She only had a second to consider how sexy that was before Jensen went to his knees, widened her stance with his hands and put his mouth over her clit.

She would've gone down in a heap if not for Tanner holding her steady against his hard chest. Tanner's mouth latched onto the side of her neck, biting her with the same intensity Jensen used on her clit.

She shot into a short, sharp orgasm, making her cry out in sheer bliss as the waves radiated throughout her body.

Her *arus* rose and this time she couldn't corral it fast enough. It burst from her and into the men, heightening their own arousal. Jensen pulled back, gasping as he stood to rip open his jeans at the same time he covered her mouth with his.

She tasted her essence on his lips as he ate at her mouth.

Behind her, she felt Tanner's hands releasing his jeans, pushing them down. She thrust her ass against him, seeking relief for the ache between her legs.

She nearly cried when Tanner lifted her hips and slid his cock into her pussy from behind. She moaned, stretched and full, her sheath clenching around him. Then he moved but not to thrust. He sat on the couch behind him, forcing her to break her connection with Jensen.

As Tanner arranged her on his lap with her legs spread and began to pump, his hands supporting her weight, Jensen pushed his jeans down and aimed his thick cock directly toward her mouth.

When he paused, as if to ask permission, she leaned forward those last few inches and sucked the tip into her mouth. She watched Jensen's eyes shut in ecstasy, felt his hands cradle her face, then he began to fuck her mouth in slow, deliberate thrusts.

Tanner fell into rhythm with Jensen, a constant thrust and retreat that set her on the fine edge of an orgasm and let her hang there, wanting to fall yet not wanting this to end.

She sucked Jensen to the back of her throat, her hands clenched around Tanner's wrists as he supported her entire weight. Pulling back, she licked the head of Jensen's cock before taking him all the way in again and swallowing. It was too much for Jensen, whose cock jerked in her mouth and began to pump his seed down her throat.

Behind her, Tanner bit her shoulder as she came, her sheath convulsing around him until he came with a groan that made her body shudder.

* * * * *

Jensen felt Nica slide from the bed, so slowly it was obvious she was trying not to make a sound.

Tanner was out cold on the far side of the bed. Unfortunately for Nica, Jensen had never been a sound sleeper. You're too damn vulnerable in sleep. He'd learned that lesson the hard way.

He didn't move but watched as she gathered her clothes, trying not to wake them. A hard knot formed in his stomach and he found it increasingly hard to keep his breathing even and regular.

Why the hell was she sneaking out of their bed in the middle of the night after mind-blowing sex?

She was hiding something. Or lying about something. Whatever it was, his bullshit meter had spiked into the red at the bar tonight. That alone should've made him take a step back, or at least slow down. Find out what was going on.

Instead they'd fallen on her like starving men at an all-you-can-eat buffet. She'd walked into the bar, crooked her finger and they'd followed her like lovesick puppies.

Okay, not exactly how it'd happened, but as he lay there watching her try to sneak out, he wondered what the fuck was going on.

The sex had been amazing. Volcano-hot and effortless. As if they'd done it before.

Which was just crazy. Yes, he and Tanner had had the same dream about her the night before. But that wasn't unprecedented. As kids, they'd often had the exact same dreams. As if their brains were somehow connected. It used to freak out their father.

They'd learned early in life not to upset Dad.

Dealing with him had also taught Jensen that lies always came back to bite you on the ass.

Faking sleep, he let her dress then sneak out of the room. When he heard her hit the squeaky step at the top of the stairs, he rolled out of bed and pulled on his jeans.

He followed her downstairs, avoiding all the noisy spots along the way, and caught up with her as she stopped beside the window, as if looking for someone. Or standing guard.

Why would she feel the need to do that?

Jensen had opened his mouth to ask when he heard her sniffle. With her back to him, he couldn't see her face but he was pretty sure she was crying.

Shit. He didn't do tears. Tanner always took care of the crying women. Tanner knew how to handle them, how to get them to stop. Jensen thought women used tears like ammunition, just another tool in their infinite box to keep men in line.

But Nica had waited to cry until she thought neither of them would hear her. She wasn't using it to manipulate them. Something had made her genuinely sad.

And his chest tightened as he watched her fumble with her purse as her shoulders shook.

Fuck it.

Walking up behind her, he put his arms around her, drawing her back against his chest. She jumped a little in his arms, startled, but didn't pull away when he put his lips next to her ear.

"Don't go."

It was the only thing he could think to say that wasn't a question she probably wouldn't answer. Or a command she wouldn't obey.

She shook her head. "I wasn't. I only wanted…" She stopped to draw in a shaky breath but didn't continue.

"You don't have to explain anything," Jensen said. "Just don't sneak out in the middle of the night. Are you okay? Are you…scared?"

She laughed, a short, sharp exhalation of air that didn't sound at all amused. "No, not scared. Not of you or Tanner."

Jensen heard a "but" in there and his arms tightened around her. If she was afraid of someone else, he wanted her to tell him who. Did she have a boyfriend who would hurt her if he found out she'd slept with them? He didn't think she did, but maybe she was afraid of her father or a brother or…

Hell, just ask her. "Do you have a boyfriend, Nica?"

She laughed again. "No. There are no men in my life."

"Then what are you afraid of?"

Her sigh shook her entire body and he had the urge to tell her he'd take care of whatever problems she had. He'd never had the desire to say that to a woman. He was no knight in shining armor.

"Losing my freedom."

His frown was immediate. "What the— Nica, are you in some kind of trouble?"

She sighed again. "No. At least, nothing I can't handle. And it's nothing you can help me with."

Fine. Everyone was entitled to their secrets. He could respect that. "Stay with us until Monday."

He swore he felt her stop breathing. Was she considering his offer? Or was she thinking about how to get out of there before he got down on one knee and proposed? Not that he'd do it. Ever. He wasn't offering anything more than a couple of nights—

"I'd like to…"

Exactly what he wanted to hear. He placed his lips on her neck, just behind her ear. God, she smelled amazing. Sweet and sexy and so damn arousing. After a brief hesitation, she pressed back into him, his hardening cock nestling into her ass.

"Do you have to work tomorrow?" he asked.

She shuddered as he licked a path from her ear to her collarbone. "No. But I'm starting a new job Monday."

His hands lifted to cup her breasts, thumbs flicking over the tight tips. "Do you have plans for tomorrow?"

Her hands came up to press against his, forcing him to curl his fingers around her breasts just a little harder. "No. No plans."

"Good."

He bit her neck, not hard enough to leave a mark but just enough to make her moan. The husky sound touched off a blast of heat in his gut, spreading down into his groin, making his cock pound for her. His arms contracted around her. He wasn't letting her go without a damn good reason.

When she pressed back into him, rubbing her tight little ass against his erection, he released his control and turned her with a growl.

Their lips met with almost punishing force and her arms wrapped around his shoulders. She pressed against him as if she were starved for him, rubbing her mound against his erection.

Rational thought fled as the heat of her body seeped into him.

Damn, he'd come in her mouth not even two hours ago but he couldn't seem to get enough of her. He had her jeans around her ankles by the time she kicked off her sandals. When he heard them hit the floor, he lifted her so her jeans could fall off as well. The sexy little motions she made to help get rid of them made it that much more imperative to get inside her.

With one arm wrapped around her waist, holding her feet off the floor, he used his other hand to rip at the button of his jeans. Lust pushed him to go faster. Before he shoved his jeans off, he walked to the couch, set her on her feet and spun her again.

He shoved his jeans to his knees as he bent her over the arm of the couch, his cock throbbing with need. Watching her hands shoot out in front of her to steady herself, he slowed long enough to make sure she was on board.

"Nica, are you—"

"Fine. I'm fine. Shut up and fuck me, Jensen."

Her husky, lust-filled voice made him feel as if she'd wrapped a hand around his dick and pumped him.

He looked down, the dim glow from the outside streetlight allowing him to just barely see the sheen of moisture on her bare flesh.

With his feet, he widened her stance until he had a better view. Her sex was still a little swollen from earlier and he used two fingers to rub along her silky skin. Wet, hot. So fucking hot.

She moaned again and wiggled her ass as his fingers slid lower, brushing over her clit.

"Jensen, please."

"Absolutely, baby. Hold on."

Taking his cock in hand, he aimed straight for her slick entrance, working himself in slow and easy. The tight fit of her pussy made him fight against the wicked urge to pound into her, to get off as hard and as fast as possible.

But he wanted to make sure she got off as well, wanted her to know what she would miss if she left. So he tunneled inside her with steady pressure as his fingers brushed over her clit.

She moaned his name as she tilted her hips, giving him more precious centimeters into her body. When he was seated fully, he stopped, absorbing the sensation. Goddamn, he wanted to stay right there, right on the brink of pleasure and pain. His body cried out for release but his soul wanted to stay wrapped around her, in her, covering her.

His.

It was that thought that pushed him over the edge. His hips reared back and he began to thrust mindlessly, lost in the pleasure and in the sound of her moans egging him on. She met each of his thrusts with her own, impaled herself on his cock as far as she could as her body began to convulse around his.

She cried out her release as he shouted his, his body tightening to the point of pain as he came in hard, pulsing bursts.

Breathing hard, he held himself inside her, loathe to move away. But if he didn't, they'd make a mess on the couch and the floor.

And Nica couldn't be comfortable, her limp body draped over that arm. Though she did have a smile on her lips.

"Here."

Turning, Jensen saw Tanner behind him, holding out a towel.

His brother was bleary eyed and shaking his head, but he wasn't angry. His expression showed tired amusement.

Had he watched? Probably. Damn, Jensen had been so far gone, he hadn't noticed Tanner at all.

"Did we wake you?"

Tanner smiled. "Not me." So yeah, he was watching. "But you probably woke the damn neighbors."

Jensen pulled back, using the towel to wipe both himself and Nica before helping her to stand.

She met first his gaze then Tanner's, biting her bottom lip. Was she afraid Tanner would be jealous?

Before Tanner could ask what they were doing down there, he rushed in to fill the silence. "Nica's going to stay until Monday."

A little more of the sleep cleared from Tanner's eyes as his smile widened. "Glad to hear it."

She frowned. "You're sure I'm not messing up any plans—"

"No plans." Tanner picked up her jeans and handed them to her, before he lifted her into his arms, startling her into a laugh. "But how about a shower then back to bed? I need a little more than an hour's worth of sleep a night. And Jensen's downright mean if he doesn't get at least seven hours."

Tanner headed for the stairs and Jensen watched Nica glance over his brother's shoulder at him. Wary, a little worried.

He grinned and followed along. She had nothing to fear. He and Tanner didn't do jealousy. At least, not of each other. She'd learn. They'd teach her.

Oh man, would they teach her.

Chapter Five

Tanner rolled out of bed Sunday morning around ten, already smiling.

He'd never felt better.

But he was hungry as hell.

A quick glance back at the bed showed Jensen and Nica still fast asleep, Jensen curled around her back, an arm and a leg thrown over as if she might get away.

They'd be hungry too, and since he was first up, he'd make breakfast. Besides, Jensen couldn't cook to save his life.

After pulling on a pair of sweats, he headed for the kitchen and pulled together the ingredients for pancakes, a smile on his face as he worked.

Last night... Hell, last night had been amazing. Nica was amazing and he'd never said that about another woman.

He'd never met a woman as sexually open or as sweet as Nica. She'd given herself over to them but hadn't simply let them have her, like some women in a threesome did. She'd participated, she'd occasionally demanded and she'd given them everything they'd asked for and more.

Just thinking about last night made his cock hard as he heated the griddle and mixed ingredients.

They still had questions, questions they needed answers to but—

"Can I give you a hand? Not that I don't love seeing a man who knows his way around a kitchen..."

Tanner turned to see Nica standing at the end of the counter, watching him with a slight smile on her lips. He hadn't heard her come downstairs but he'd turned on the radio on the counter.

Her hair was mussed and fell in long, wavy strands around her shoulders. She wore Tanner's Oxford shirt from last night, which was long enough to cover her almost to her knees.

She looked a little sleepy and a whole lot sexy and before he realized what he meant to do, he put down the whisk and the bowl and walked over to her.

Threading one hand through her hair, he dropped his mouth on hers for a rough, quick kiss. Not long enough to make him forget what he was doing, just enough to let her know he was happy to see her.

Which she could probably tell from the tent in the front of his sweats.

"I've got this under control. But I like company."

Putting his hands around her waist, he lifted her onto the counter, close enough to touch but far enough away from the hot griddle. She gasped then laughed as she worked the shirt down under her bare ass, giving him a quick glimpse of the small triangle of curls on her mound.

Fuck breakfast. He'd rather have her. But she needed to eat. "Hope you like pancakes."

"I love pancakes." She paused as she watched him. "Are you sure you don't mind the company for today? I mean, if you have something better—"

"Believe it or not, honey, there's absolutely nothing I'd rather do than spend today with you." He slid a quick glance at her as he ladled pancake batter onto the hot surface. "I just hope you don't find us too boring. We're not exactly party animals."

Which was probably truer than anything else he'd said. He and Jensen usually spent weekends working on the house, catching up on paperwork for the business or hanging out with friends.

They'd converted the basement into a man cave, complete with a home entertainment system, including a Wii and an Xbox, a card table, a vintage pinball machine and a sound system that could rattle pictures off the walls upstairs.

"Neither am I." She paused again. "I'm not…I don't normally do this. Spend the weekend with a guy I just met. Or two guys for that matter."

He slid her a glance. "You're not uncomfortable, are you? Because—"

She laughed, the husky sound rasping over his nerves. "Not uncomfortable, not at all. It's just…" Sighing, she shook her head. "My life is about to change drastically and I feel like I can't enjoy this too much because… Because I'll never be able to have it again."

Moving the first batch of pancakes off the griddle, he turned it off and gave her his full attention. He'd finish them later. There was something in Nica's tone, something that made him think this woman was in trouble. And Tanner never turned away a damsel in distress.

Stepping over to her, he put his hands on either side of her hips and stared straight into those dark brown eyes.

"Are you in trouble, Nica?"

Nica's lips quirked into a quick grin and she lifted one hand to Tanner's cheek, rubbing her palm against his dark gold morning stubble, wondering what he'd do if she told him exactly what was going on in her life.

That she was a *strega*, a witch who could read auras and work spells. That two nights ago, she'd wiped his and his brother's memories clean after a madman had almost kidnapped her and killed Jensen.

"What would you do if I told you I was?"

His expression never changed. "I'd find a way to get you out of it."

Her smile widened. "Wouldn't that be nice? A knight in shining armor."

Who would think she was crazy if she told him her trouble. But she so needed someone to talk to. "It's my work situation. I'm changing positions on Monday and I'm not sure it's what I want to do."

"Is it mandatory?"

"Yes."

He shrugged naked, broad shoulders. "So renegotiate the terms of your contract. If they want to keep you, they'll find a way to make it work for you. Does this job require you to move?"

Did he sound unhappy about that? Would he and Jensen want to continue see her after this weekend? Wouldn't it be wonderful if they could?

Not going to happen.

She nodded. "Not far but my li—time won't be my own."

His gaze narrowed. "Are you sure you want this job? I think you should seriously consider quitting and finding another one, especially if it makes you this miserable."

Looking into Tanner's pale blue eyes, Nica wished it were that easy.

As she stroked her fingers along his jaw, she thought about how his rough whiskers would feel against her naked breasts.

She swallowed hard as desire flooded through her body and her lungs suddenly struggled to draw in air. After last night, she would've thought she'd be sexually satisfied, at least for the morning.

But she wanted him. Tanner and his brother had unlocked a sensuality she hadn't known she possessed. Or maybe it was her way of staving off the desperation she felt whenever she thought about taking over her mom's position in the *boschetta*.

At this moment, it didn't matter because Tanner's eyes narrowed down to slits of pale blue. His hands settled on her bare knees for a brief second before beginning a slow slide under her shirt and up her thighs.

His head lowered as if he were going to kiss her but he diverted at the last second to lay his lips along her jaw. He nipped her, a tiny bite that stung just as his fingers tunneled between her thighs to stroke the hair on her mound.

She drew in a sharp breath as every muscle in her body tightened with heated lust.

Her hand on his cheek slid back into his short-cropped hair while her other landed on his waist, just above his sweatpants. His warm skin felt like silk and she traced the elastic waistband around to the front before sliding her fingers beneath it.

His indrawn breath against her ear made her smile as she brushed against the tip of his cock, eliciting a shudder from him.

"Nica."

"Hmm."

He kissed her then, his lips opening over hers and taking her down. His tongue slid into her mouth, enticing her with quick jabs and thrusts as his hands slowly spread her legs. The shirt she wore rode up her thighs, higher and higher until she felt the slightly cooler air of the kitchen brush against the bare, aching flesh of her pussy.

He had to be able to smell her desire. She could. Did it make him as horny as it did her?

Her fingers wrapped around his cock and squeezed. He groaned into her mouth before pulling his lips away but keeping his hands right where she wanted them.

"I want you." His voice rumbled from his chest, making her sex tighten and ache.

"Then take me, Tanner."

A second later, his fingers arrowed in on her clit, rubbing the little bundle of nerves with a steady motion that had her panting in seconds.

Her head fell back, resting against the cabinet behind her, and she moaned in surrender. She spread her legs even farther, letting Tanner get closer.

His fingers withdrew as his hips pressed in, still confined by his sweats.

Without releasing her hold around his cock, she grabbed his sweats in her other hand and shoved them down his thighs. He stopped for a brief second, breathing hard, his eyes burning into hers, questioning.

She didn't want questions. She wanted oblivion. She released him and grabbed his hips.

"Tanner, please. Just—"

He thrust hard as he pulled her forward, filling her completely and making her moan.

Wrapping one arm around her, he held her steady as he fucked her with an almost uncontrolled passion. One hand snaked into her hair, forcing her head forward so he could put his mouth over hers and ravage that along with her body.

The roughness of the act made her heart race. She gave herself up to it and let him have her.

Her sex, already tight from last night's activities, felt every thrust and retreat of his cock with heightened sensitivity. She soaked up the sensation of his skin dragging against hers, let the slight pinch of overworked flesh keep her on the edge of orgasm.

She couldn't seem to get enough air with Tanner's insistent mouth over hers but the oxygen deprivation only made her hotter.

As her body strained toward climax, Tanner's harsh groans answered her sobbing moans.

Finally, she snapped, her womb convulsing and sending devastating waves of pleasure through her body. She pulled away from his kiss to gasp in air and felt Tanner's cock jerk and pump his seed into her.

She held onto him as her body struggled to regain equilibrium. Instead of feeling tired, she felt energized, electricity shooting through her body with little zings.

Tanner's heavy breathing brushed her ear for several long seconds until he finally stopped pulsing in her and lifted his head.

"Good morning to you too," he said, dropping a quick kiss on her forehead before pulling back to look at her with a grin. "I think I better make more food. We're gonna need to keep up our strength."

* * * * *

Jensen walked into the kitchen a half hour later, took one look at Tanner and knew his brother had had Nica this morning.

They sat at the table in the kitchen, reading the paper and eating pancakes, but the smile on Tanner's face revealed more than the headlines.

Nica looked bright-eyed and flushed, a patch of beard burn on her jaw from Tanner's stubble. Oh yeah. They'd had sex.

Jensen stifled a grin. Hell, if they had to fuck her constantly today, it'd be worth it to keep her there. He'd gladly go to work catatonic on Monday.

"Did you leave me any food or do I have to fend for myself?"

Tanner didn't bother to look up, just waved his fork toward the oven.

"I put aside a plate for you," Nica said, her smile warm. "Otherwise, Tanner would've eaten yours."

Jensen walked to the oven and liberated his still-hot plate before sitting down across from Nica. "Yeah, he's a pig."

Tanner snorted. "Who got up and cooked? Me, as usual. You'd starve if left to your own devices."

"Bullshit. I can feed myself. That's why God created take-out. But why should I bother when you're so good in the kitchen?"

Tanner flipped him the bird, his gaze still hooked on the paper. But Nica's laugh tore it away.

"Have you two always bickered like this?"

Jensen shrugged as he dumped syrup on his pancakes. "Pretty much."

"Kinda comes with the territory." Tanner put the paper down. "Don't you have any brothers or sisters?"

Jensen forced himself to continue eating, even though he wanted to stop and force her to answer. He had a burning urge to know everything about this woman and he knew Tanner would too.

After a brief pause, she set her fork down and reached for a napkin from the pile in the center of the table. "I'm an only child. Just me and my mom but I never lacked for friends. I grew up in a…small town where there were lots of girls my age. My best friend, Tira, is my sister in every way but blood. We're living together now but…not for long. I'm moving next weekend."

Jensen's head shot up. "Where are you going?"

She blinked, like a deer caught in the headlights. "Not far, actually. But I'll be…out of touch for a while. Several weeks, actually. Training for my new position is intensive."

Tanner leaned back in his chair, his laidback attitude casually deceptive. "You work in a doctor's office now, right? Is your new job in healthcare?"

She nodded. "Yes, just not with the same company."

Tanner nodded, as if he bought her explanation. He didn't. Neither did Jensen. More secrets. This woman had a ton of them. And they'd asked her to stay in their house for the weekend.

But Jensen knew, absolutely, that she posed no threat to them. She was there for one thing only—the sex. She wasn't a thief or a con artist. She wasn't a psycho.

She was sweet and hot and she was telling them, without words, that she would never see them again after this weekend.

And that was not what he wanted to hear.

He opened his mouth to ask her flat out what was going on but Tanner, probably knowing exactly what he wanted to say, cut him off.

"So do you want us to run you home for some clothes or do you prefer to wear as little as possible? I have to say I prefer the latter."

Nica laughed, genuinely amused, her smile bright and warm. "If you don't mind me raiding your closets, then I think I'll be fine."

"We don't mind," Jensen answered. "At all."

Anything to keep her there.

* * * * *

They finished breakfast and wouldn't let her help with the dishes, so Nica sat and watched them.

It didn't take them long to clean up because they knew exactly what the other would do. They had a system, she realized. They worked together well, which she knew from having them in bed together.

Just thinking about last night made her body heat. She wanted them again. Damn, maybe she was turning into a nymphomaniac. She wondered if that would toss her out of the running for the *boschetta*.

Wishful thinking.

She stifled a sigh but Jensen chose that moment to look at her and his gaze narrowed as if he'd read her mind. She smiled at him as he bent to put the last plate in the dishwasher. She'd have to watch him. He was almost preternaturally perceptive.

She knew Tanner had questions too, but Jensen sensed more of her feelings. She heard it in the tone of his questions and saw it in his expression.

She hated lying to these two wonderful men, truly wished she could spill her heart and her troubles at their feet. She'd only had Tira to complain to and Tira was too close to the situation to give her some much needed perspective.

"So, Nica," Tanner interrupted her train of thought as he tossed the dishtowel on the counter and walked back to the table. "How's your 'Guitar Hero'?"

"Can't say I've ever actually played." She smiled. "But I'm willing to learn."

Tanner held out his hand. "Then come with me."

Putting her hand in his, she let him lead her through the house to a stairwell into the basement.

As the light flipped on, she smiled at the overt masculinity of their grown-up playroom.

A huge TV hung on one long wall, the shelves beneath filled with electronic equipment, DVDs and speakers.

An enormous, leather, U-shaped couch faced the TV and Tanner picked up a remote the size of a paperback book from one of the cushions. After he pressed a few buttons, lights flashed on several pieces on the shelves and the TV hummed to life.

Half an hour later, Nica stood in front of the TV holding a plastic guitar in her hand and laughing so hard she had tears in her eyes. Tanner's fingers flew over the neck of his guitar as Van Halen's "Hot for Teacher" pounded out of the speakers.

"You know, I can type a hundred words a minute but I can't press three little buttons in succession." She shook her head as she tried to get her fingers to press the buttons in the correct order. "I can't believe this game is so hard."

She tossed a look over her shoulder at Jensen, lounging on the couch behind her. His amused grin nearly took her breath away and stole her concentration away from the little bars and notes on the screen she was supposed to be following.

"Don't be too hard on yourself," Jensen said. "Tanner's a geek. He's addicted to this game. He must play at least two hours a day."

"Stress relief." Tanner's fingers kept moving with the game, even as he looked at her and winked. "It's mindless and it's got good music."

"And you're constantly complaining about wanker's cramp."

"That…sounds dirty and disturbing," Nica said as she tried to follow along with the game. Hell, she was playing on easy mode and it was too hard for her.

Both men laughed.

"It just means his hands cramp up from playing the game too much," Jensen said. "Although…"

"Yeah, well, Jensen's just jealous," Tanner said. "I beat him every time."

"Because you're a geek with no life."

Nica laughed so hard she couldn't keep up and passed the guitar to Jensen for the next song. He took it with a wink as she curled into a corner of the couch, watching the brothers battle each other. They both displayed an intense concentration that reminded her of their complete concentration on her pleasure in bed.

Her gaze fell on Tanner, his fingers moving with a light touch over the keys, his head bobbing to the music and his feet tapping on the floor. The slight smile on his face as he hit every note made her remember the expression on his face this morning when she'd come in his arms—utter satisfaction that he'd brought her to that point.

Her sheath clenched and her nipples tightened under the shirt she wore.

Was sex all she was going to think about the entire time she was there? And would that be such a bad thing?

Her gaze shifted to Jensen. He wasn't smiling. His gaze narrowed, his fingers worked the keys at a steady pace. He missed more notes than Tanner and every time he did, he bit his bottom lip and his gaze narrowed even more.

She wanted to bite his bottom lip. She wanted Tanner's fingers to play over her clit with that lightning-fast touch.

Okay, she *was* becoming a nympho. But really, when would she have this opportunity again? Two gorgeous men at her beck and call for a whole day.

Her lungs struggled for air as she began to unbutton her shirt. Her free hand reached behind her for a pillow to prop her head on as she continued to watch the guys.

With the shirt unbuttoned, she let her hand slip beneath the fabric to tweak her sensitive nipples. Neither man wore a shirt and the sleek muscles of their backs and arms rippled as they played.

Heat spilled through her blood, lust hard on its heels. Her hand stroked her breasts, plumping and kneading. Her sex contracted, needing to be filled again.

Breathing more heavily now, she let her hand slide down her stomach, felt the muscles tighten. When her fingers brushed against the trimmed hair on her mound, she saw Jensen's hands falter on the guitar.

Her lips parted to draw in much needed air and Jensen turned his head as if he'd heard her, though how he could over the loud music was a mystery.

His gaze met hers for a brief second before arrowing down to her hand at her mound. He watched as she slid her hand between her thighs, her fingers playing over her clit. The sensation made her wet, heightened by Jensen's gaze.

With a final burst of guitars, the song came to an end and Tanner hit Jensen on the shoulder.

"Dude," Tanner said, "you— Oh fuck."

Tanner's gaze caught and held on Nica as she pushed her fingers even farther between her legs, coating her fingers in the juices spilling from her sex.

Her eyes closed as fierce bolts of electricity shot through her womb. Her lips parted on a silent moan as she rubbed the moisture over her swollen, aching flesh.

The couch dipped at her feet and above her head as the guys moved in on her. Jensen's large, warm hands landed heavy on her thighs just above her knees then slid upward, pushing her legs apart as they went.

Tanner took her hand from beneath the pillow and raised it toward him. Her knuckles met worn denim and behind it, the hard ridge of his erection. Opening her hand, she molded her fingers to him as Jensen kneaded her thighs, his hands moving closer and closer to where she needed them.

As she stroked Tanner through his jeans, his hands cupped her breasts, thumbs flicking over the nipples, diamond-hard and begging for a firmer touch.

She moaned as she felt the couch shift and Jensen's breath blew across her pussy, causing her muscles to tense with anticipation. Her legs tried to close, to trap him between them but he held her open as his tongue swiped across her clit with flat, broad strokes.

The hand she'd used to play with herself tangled in Jensen's hair and held him to her. Her other hand tightened on Tanner's cock until he groaned then she released him to fumble blindly with the zipper. He hadn't buttoned them, thank the Blessed Goddess, or she might've gone mad trying to undo it one-handed.

She still might lose her sanity, she decided, when Tanner moved and his lips sucked one tight nipple into his hot mouth.

The brothers' tongues stroked and swiped at odd rhythms, the maddening sensations causing her body to go on sensory overload.

Her hand finally released Tanner's cock from his jeans and somehow she got him positioned correctly to take into her mouth.

Soft, silky skin slid past her lips and into her mouth, the male scent of him intensified by the lack of sight. The angle of penetration forced his cock to sink deeper, her tongue to stroke at a different angle. Tanner's strangled groan vibrated through her, his teeth nicking her nipple and causing her body to bow off the couch.

Jensen's hands slid to her hips to hold her down and with Tanner above her, she felt enclosed, almost trapped. She liked it, enjoyed the sense of being taken out of herself until she was reduced to a creature of pure desire.

Jensen's teeth took little bites of her labia before licking away the hurt and thrusting his tongue into her sheath. And pressing one lubricated finger against her tight back entrance.

Oh yes. Gods, yes, she wanted both.

Her legs spread and she thrust her hips up as far as Jensen would let her, trying to show her complete acquiescence to his wordless question.

Jensen reared back as his finger plunged deeper, setting off tremors through her body. Where he'd gotten the lube, she had no idea, but she was thankful for it. It'd been at least a year since she'd indulged in this particular pleasure and she'd never had two men at the same time.

But she couldn't wait.

Pulling away from Tanner, with one final lick to the end of his cock, she opened her eyes and looked down at Jensen, staring intently at her as he worked his finger slowly in and out of her back entrance.

He wasn't asking this time. He already knew her answer. Behind her, Tanner shifted out of her line of vision but her entire focus was on Jensen right now.

He stroked her, watched her with those pale blue eyes, drinking in her every trembling breath.

Her body loosened and he worked in another finger, heightening her pleasure until she thought she might pass out. Devastating mini-orgasms arced through her body and her eyes closed in sheer bliss.

Then she was moving.

Jensen lifted her off the couch as Tanner repositioned himself on the cushions, flat on his back. Twisting her around, Jensen maneuvered her body until she faced Tanner, her knees sinking into the cushions on either side of him.

Without thought, she reached for Tanner's cock and aimed it straight into her wet slit, sinking onto his hard shaft with a grateful sigh. Tanner reached for her, curled his arms around her shoulders and brought her down to lie against his chest.

Her lips sought his for a drugging kiss, sucking on his tongue when he forced it into her mouth.

Behind her, she felt Jensen's slick cock press against the puckered rim of her ass and she pushed back against him, inviting him in.

Tanner lay still beneath her, waiting as Jensen worked his cock into her, a centimeter at a time.

The sense of fullness made her gasp, her mouth tearing away from Tanner's to draw in much-needed air.

Behind her, Jensen froze. "Nica, are—"

"Oh Gods, don't stop now," she begged. "Jensen…Tanner, please."

Jensen forged ahead with a groan, still moving too slowly for her. She wanted…had to have motion, friction.

This terrible, wonderful need eating her from the inside needed to be fed. She pushed back just the tiniest bit and Jensen bit off a rough sound.

And lodged his cock to the hilt in her ass.

For several seconds, no one moved. Tanner's breath sawed roughly by her ear and Jensen's hands on her hips dug in so hard, it was almost painful. A good pain.

Just like the biting stretch of her ass and her pussy.

It was good, so good.

And then it got better. Tanner pulled back, his cock hitting every nerve ending and sending waves of pleasure through her. When he thrust back in, Jensen began to pull out.

They set up a wicked, rough rhythm. Nothing about it was smooth and she wanted to move but she didn't know how. She let them take her, let them fuck her between them, let them take her over the top.

She tried to hold back her orgasm, to hold herself on the edge of it as long as she could but the feeling they produced was too good.

Her body tensed a millisecond before her sheath convulsed in an almost painful orgasm that made her pussy and her ass contract around the cocks stretching them, made the men groan out their pleasure as they jerked and pulsed their cum into her.

Each tiny ripple of their cocks prolonged her orgasm until she felt she couldn't stand any more and she let her body go limp as ecstasy overwhelmed her.

Tanner felt a tight knot in the center of his chest as he tried to catch his breath.

Arousal still zinged through his body after that orgasm had rocked him.

Nica shuddered on top of him as Jensen pulled out of her and Tanner held her even more tightly.

The couch shifted and Jensen sank into the cushions at Tanner's feet, his brother's breathing so rough, Tanner could hear him over his own.

He wasn't sure if Nica was still awake or if she'd passed out.

Christ, he'd almost blacked out. It'd never been that good before. He'd never come that hard, not with any of the other women he and Jensen had shared. And there'd been several.

So what was it about this one?

And why did he care?

He never psychoanalyzed. That was Jensen's deal. Jen was like a dog with a bone when he worked stuff over in his head.

Tanner refused to drive himself crazy with what-ifs. Shit happened. Most of the time, you couldn't control it, so why get worked up over it?

Still, Nica was different. He wanted to get into her head, know what was going on. Know what she was trying to hide from them and why.

He wanted to dig around in his own head and figure out why he knew his feelings for her were different from any other woman he'd ever known.

And he wanted to know if Jensen felt the same.

His gaze flashed to his brother, sitting at the far end of the couch, eyes closed.

Though not for long. Jensen's eyes flashed open as if he'd felt Tanner looking at him and they exchanged a glance that told Tanner all he needed to know about what his brother was thinking.

Exactly the same thing.

She'd given them today. And tomorrow, she'd said, she was starting a new job and would be unavailable for months.

What the hell kind of job was that? And why wouldn't she tell them more?

Something didn't ring true. Not that he didn't trust her. Hell, he trusted her enough to have sex without a condom, which was a huge leap for him, even with the medical report. Same for Jensen.

And she'd trusted them as well. At least with her body.

Tanner wanted to know more. He knew Jensen did too. But if they continued like this, none of them would have enough strength to ask questions between all the sex. And maybe that was exactly the way she wanted it.

"Hmm, I think I could sleep right here, but I don't think your couch will ever be the same if we don't get up soon."

Nica's husky voice penetrated deep into Tanner's chest, wrapping around his lungs and squeezing. Hell, with very little effort he could probably get it up again and that would be a fucking miracle, considering.

"Leather cleans up easy, baby." Jensen chuckled. "Now you know our dirty little secret."

Nica chuckled and damn if his cock didn't twitch.

"Glad to hear it." Her hands flexed against Tanner's chest. "Now, though, I think I need a shower."

"Then your wish is our command." Jensen stood and lifted her into his arms, Tanner's skin registering the loss by breaking out in gooseflesh. "Tanner'll find you something to wear."

As his brother disappeared up the stairs with Nica, Tanner sat up slowly.

She trusted them enough to let them into her body in such intimate ways and yet she wouldn't tell them what was going on in her life.

That was going to change. Tanner wanted answers. And he wanted them now.

Chapter Six

"Nica, are you okay?"

Tira's voice sounded wary, a little frightened, and Nica's chest immediately constricted with worry.

With Tanner upstairs getting dressed and Jensen in the basement, Nica had locked herself in the powder room off the kitchen to return Tira's message from an hour ago.

"I'm fine, Tira. Did something happen?"

Tira sighed, a little weary, a little confused. "I had a vision, a pretty indistinct one. I saw you, crying, worried. I don't know where you were. I didn't recognize your surroundings. Nica, I've never had a vision like that. It was almost like," she sighed again, "like someone was deliberately messing with it, making it fuzzy."

"What do you think it means?"

"I don't know. I do know I've had this weird anxiety all day, like something was going to happen but I didn't know what or when or to whom. Are you sure you're okay?"

"I'm fine, T, really. Better than fine."

"Ooh, now that sounds interesting." Tira's tone lightened considerably. "I'm going to want lots of details when you—"

Tira paused and for a second Nica thought the phone went dead.

"T, are you there?"

"Yeah, I thought I saw— Hold on a sec. Someone's at the door."

Nica heard Tira put the phone down and walk to the door. Their apartment door opened with its distinctive squeak...

And Tira's scream ricocheted through the phone for one brief, terrifying second before it cut off.

"Tira! Oh Gods, Tira! What's—"

"Hello again, Niccola."

Fear seeped through Nica's veins like ice as she recognized the voice of the man who'd attacked them the other night.

"You! What have you done to Tira?"

"Your friend is fine and will remain fine. As long as we hear from you tomorrow. Your roommate is our insurance. You don't have to worry about her health. We just want you to make the right decision, Nica. Come Monday, when we contact you again, she'll be released."

"Please, just let her go now," Nica begged.

"She'll be fine. And Monday, when you come to work for us, she will be returned safe and sound. You have my word."

"That's not worth much after the other night. You nearly killed him."

"But you had the power to heal him, Nica. Apparently you did such a great job that he's had no trouble performing. You and the brothers having a good time?"

"You bastard—"

"You have until Monday morning, Nica. I'll be back in touch."

The phone went dead.

"Wait!"

Blessed Goddess. That madman had Tira. And it was all her fault.

She needed to contact Sal, needed to call Teo and his brother Cam to find Tira. She opened the door—

And ran into the arms of two scowling men.

"Nica." Tanner's tone held absolutely no give. "What's going on?"

She wanted to tell them. Blessed Goddess, she wanted to confide in them, didn't want to have secrets between them. But they'd never believe her.

Unless she gave them back their memories from the night before.

Looking into their eyes, she saw their concern for her, their need to know and to help. They were good men and in another time and place, she could love men like this.

So not fair...

What would they do if she told them everything?

Would they believe her?

"Nica." Tanner's voice soothed jangled nerves. "Come on, babe. It can't be that bad. We only want to help."

But they couldn't. They had no magic to protect themselves.

And aren't you putting them in even more danger by not *telling them exactly why you're in danger?*

Of course, she was. They deserved to know. And if they couldn't handle it, she'd bring in someone more powerful to wipe their memories, for good this time. Which she'd have to do Monday anyway.

A sharp pain in her chest made her gulp in air. "I'll tell you what's going on but... It's going to sound crazy. You're going to think I'm nuts and I'm not, just... Please, keep an open mind."

Jensen's gaze narrowed even further. She knew he was the one who would have the most trouble with what she was going to tell them. Tanner would shake his head and smile but when she demonstrated her power, he'd believe her.

She'd show them what they didn't know about the world. And when this situation was over, their memories would be erased. And she'd disappear from their lives.

* * * * *

Nica had been right, Jensen decided.

He thought she was crazy.

For the past ten minutes, as they sat at the kitchen table, she'd gone on about how she was a descendent of the ancient Etruscan magical races, a *strega*, otherwise known as a witch, and that she could perform magic.

"You really believe you're a witch?" Jensen slid a glance at Tanner, trying to gauge his brother's thoughts, but Jensen couldn't tell what Tanner was thinking. "And you really expect us to believe you."

Nica nodded, her expression as serious as a heart attack. "Yes, and I can show you."

"You can do magic?"

She shook her head. "Not sleight-of-hand. Not parlor tricks. My particular Goddess Gift is healing."

She turned to Tanner. "You saw me heal Jensen two nights ago. He was attacked by the man who's holding my friend hostage. I wiped those memories from your mind and—"

"Not completely," Tanner said.

Jensen whipped around to look at his brother. "What the hell are you talking about?"

"The dream we shared, there was more to mine." Tanner didn't look at him. He kept his gaze locked with Nica's. "Your hands glowed. What happened to Jensen?"

"He was struck with a spell, one that attempted to shut down his internal organs. I was able to heal him. Then I performed a spell that took away your memories of me. Obviously, I messed that one up. I think…because I didn't want you to forget me."

Jensen shook his head, even though he heard the sincerity in her voice. She believed every word she was saying. And Tanner did too.

"No. No way."

"Go ahead," Tanner continued to address Nica. "Show him."

With a sigh, she nodded, got up and walked to the sink, where a sharp knife lay drying on the drain board. Before he realized what she meant to do with it, she sliced her arm.

"Jesus Christ! Nica, what the fuck are you doing?"

Jensen's chair toppled as he rose and stalked to the sink. He grabbed her throbbing arm and held it over the sink.

"You see the cut." Nicas spoke so quietly, he had to strain to hear it. "You see I'm bleeding and it's no trick?"

"Christ almighty, you're going to need stitches, Nica. Why the hell—"

"No, I won't. Do you see, Jensen?"

Yes, he saw. The wound was real. Thick red blood welled on her arm and fell to the sink with distinctive little plops on the stainless steel. Her flesh peeled back on each side of the wound. She'd cut fairly deep and would need stitches—

"Watch," she said.

Nica placed her hand over the cut, her eyes closing as she went completely still.

And her hand began to glow. An ethereal blue, like someone was shining a flashlight through her skin. Jensen released her, his hands falling to his side as he watched.

She held it there for several long seconds and, when she removed her hand, the cut was gone.

"Holy shit." He took one step back before he forced himself to hold his ground.

With jerky movements, she flipped on the water and washed her trembling hands then splashed away the blood in the sink.

With a ragged deep breath, as if she had to work up the courage, Nica looked him straight in the eyes, her expression stoic but the pleading in her gaze killed him. She was waiting for him to refute her yet wanted so much for him to believe her.

Jensen was no fool. He'd seen the cut. She hadn't faked it.

He glanced at Tanner, his arms crossed over his chest, his expression somewhere between "Holy shit" and "I told you".

This woman—

No, this wasn't just some woman. This was Nica. She hadn't turned into a monster in the past ten minutes. She was still the same sweet, hot woman he'd fallen for. And he'd fallen. Hard. Those feelings hadn't changed because she had an ability that wouldn't be out of place in an Alan Moore graphic novel.

And he knew Tanner's feelings hadn't changed either. Because Jensen could sense how his brother felt.

Some people might call that magic. Their father had never believed them, had called them freaks—and worse.

Nica could heal with her hands. Yeah, it was weird. But she healed. She wasn't a monster. She wasn't a freak.

He would deal.

Behind Nica, Tanner drew in a deep breath, as if he'd been frozen, waiting for Jensen to make up his mind.

Nica still looked worried, her teeth lodged in her bottom lip, so hard he thought she might draw blood.

He reached out to cup her cheek, sliding his thumb across her bottom lip until she released it.

"Tell me about the other night," he said. "You said someone attacked me? And you wiped my—our memories with a magical spell?"

She nodded slowly, her gaze still wary, making him feel guilty for his initial disbelief.

She'd have to cut him some slack. This was an admittedly huge development to comprehend. But one he found fascinating.

"Yes. His employer wants me to work for him. He knows what I can do. I don't know how they found out but my people are very careful to keep our powers hidden from the *eteri*."

"And that means regular humans, right?" Tanner asked.

She flashed Tanner a smile that quickly faded. "I need to contact someone who can track down Tira. But I want you both to know what's going on. I'm afraid if Tira is rescued, that man will come after you. You're both in danger only because I selfishly gave in to my desire. You need to know what's going on and because I wanted to offer you protection at a safe house until this situation is resolved."

Jensen opened his mouth to say they didn't need protection but Tanner beat him to the punch. With the complete opposite reaction.

"We'll go right now," his brother said. "Why don't you go upstairs and change, Nica. Jensen and I will take you to this safe house. And we'll stay."

Nica visibly relaxed and Jensen realized why Tanner had agreed. He wanted Nica in this safe house as well. Good thing one of them was on their game.

Shutting his mouth, Jensen headed upstairs as Nica gathered her clothes from the first-floor bedroom. Tanner followed him a few seconds later.

At the top of the steps, Tanner shook his head, just once, and headed for his own bedroom.

Fine. They wouldn't discuss this. Not now, anyway.

* * * * *

Tanner drove, following Nica's directions back into the city.

They turned south on Penn then headed east into a part of the city he didn't know well. Tiny streets and alleys laced through an older neighborhood filled with townhomes and small businesses.

Finally, Nica had him park on a one-way street lined with three-story brick row houses.

As he shut off the SUV, Tanner took a look through the front window. Most of the houses were in decent repair. Only a few derelict properties stood out. Not a bad neighborhood. Not a great one either.

Before Jensen could get his door open, Nica practically flew out of the vehicle and headed straight to one of the houses that stood out in no way from the others.

Tanner slid out slowly as Jensen followed on Nica's heels. His brother only had eyes for Nica. Tanner took it slower, checking out their surroundings, noticing the faint but elaborate decoration on the wood trim around the front door.

Nica knocked once before pulling out a key from her back pocket, an old skeleton key that she fit into the lock and turned.

The door swung open soundlessly and she waved them into a small foyer.

The house looked…normal. Maybe stuck in an eighties' time warp but…

He didn't know what he'd been expecting but normal hadn't occurred to him.

Even the dark-haired kid walking down the stairs directly in front of them was normal. He looked to be ten or eleven, with a knit cap pulled down over his ears.

"Hey, Nica, how's it going? Everything okay?"

The kid eyed them with intelligent dark eyes, hands stuffed in the pockets of his jeans, a black Rolling Stones concert t-shirt hanging off thin shoulders.

Nica audibly sighed at the sight of the kid and Tanner's gaze narrowed.

"Sal, the man from the other night took Tira. He called this morning to tell me. This is Tanner and Jensen Miller. I've told them who and what I am. I told them what happened Friday night and…and I'd like you to offer them sanctuary until this situation is under control."

She turned and glanced at each of them in turn. "Jensen, Tanner, this is Salvatorus. He runs this house."

Tanner's eyes widened for a brief second. This kid ran the safe house? What the hell was going on?

Tanner turned to find Jensen looking at him, the same questions in his eyes, before Jensen moved to put himself in front of Nica. Tanner moved behind her, putting his hand on her shoulder and trying to draw her back against him. Shielding her.

Sal's head tilted to the side, as if contemplating Nica's request before he started to grin. The kid checked out Jensen first, looking him over from head to toe. Then his gaze connected with Tanner. Holy hell, the kid's eyes…

Tanner's spine stiffened in reaction. This was no kid.

"You think they can handle it, sweetheart?"

Nica nodded, though she didn't move from behind Jensen. Tanner had the feeling she was humoring them, making them feel...useful.

"Handle what?" Jensen said for both of them.

"Who Sal really is," Nica answered. "I know you've already seen what I can do, but Sal is...special."

"And she don't mean short-bus special, kids." Sal snorted, his voice seeming to deepen with a sarcastic edge. But the look he gave Nica was almost apologetic. "Niccola. I don't want you to get hurt, babe. And this has the makings of heartbreak written all over it."

"We would never hurt her," Jensen spoke before Tanner could open his mouth, saying exactly what Tanner had been thinking. "And we don't want to see Nica get hurt."

Sal must've caught Jensen's undertone because he smiled. And his image went blurry.

Tanner blinked, thinking he must have gotten something in his eyes. They didn't hurt or burn or feel gritty. The kid's whole body just blurred.

And then his vision cleared.

And instead of a child, something else stood there.

Something with the upper body of a man and the lower body of...

Tanner blinked and sucked in a deep breath, feeling like he'd been gut-punched.

"Holy fuck." Jensen's muttered curse left him no doubt that his brother felt the same.

The...whatever he was smiled, a hint of pity in it. "When they catch their breath, bring them back to the kitchen, hon." Sal clomped down the stairs, his hooves—Jesus Christ, he had hooves. "I'll get some coffee on."

Tanner tracked the thing as it walked down the hall and through the room beyond before disappearing through a doorway.

His mouth opened then closed. He didn't have a clue what to say.

Luckily Jensen recovered faster. He turned to stare at her, his eyes wide but not afraid. "Jesus Christ, Nica, is that a fucking satyr?"

Satyr. Yeah, that was the word Tanner had been trying to dig out of his non-functioning brain.

"In English, yes. In Italian, his proper designation is *salbinelli*." Nica caught her bottom lip between her teeth again before she continued. "He's one of the most brilliant men I've ever known. He's also one of the kindest."

Jensen started to shake his head and couldn't seem to stop. "Nica, that…that guy looks like he jumped off an ancient Roman tomb painting."

Nica nodded. "Yes, he does."

"How long has he lived in Reading?" Tanner asked. It was the only question that came to mind. It didn't matter one good goddamn in the whole scheme of things but… Holy shit.

"A couple of centuries at least. No one knows for sure. He's always been here."

Tanner's mouth dropped open as did Jensen's. But neither of them could come up with anything.

Then Jensen's head started to shake again but the look on his face… Jensen's gaze slid past Nica toward the back of the house. He wanted to go talk to the goat man.

Tanner had a brief flash of the bookcases in Jensen's room, filled with fantasy and sci-fi books. Jensen had always loved those genres. Meeting a creature—no, Nica had been very specific when she'd called him a man. Meeting a man who seemed to have stepped off the pages of one of his books must seem like a dream come true for Jensen.

Tanner wanted to doubt his eyes but he couldn't. Not with Jensen nearly salivating to go talk to the thing. No, to the guy. A guy with goat legs.

Ooh-kay.

"Tanner."

Nica's soft voice pulled him out of his thoughts and he looked into her dark eyes. Worry made little lines around her eyes and he lifted his hand to rub his thumb over them, trying to wipe them away.

He didn't want her to worry about him. She had enough to deal with right now. But holy shit—

No. Suck it up.

"I'm fine, Nica, but I could use the caffeine. And Jensen is dying to talk to your…friend."

"I'm sorry I got you both wrapped up in this." She shook her head. "I never wanted either of you to get hurt."

"We're fine. Really. Yeah, it's…kind of a shock to realize—" He stopped, not knowing where to go with that. Not knowing what he could say that wouldn't make her feel worse. He saw remorse in her expression and he hated it.

Christ, Jensen was chomping at the bit to go interrogate the satyr and he wanted to run the other way.

Which he wasn't about to do. If he walked out, Nica would follow him. And there was no way he wanted her to leave, if this place really was as safe as she said it was. She was in danger so she had to stay here.

And since Sal apparently knew everything, Tanner needed to talk to the guy with the hooves.

* * * * *

Jensen knew Tanner was having problems coping. Hell, it wasn't every day you met a creature out of mythology.

But from the moment Nica had revealed her powers, Jensen felt like he'd been invited into the best secret in the world. The fact that Nica felt safe enough with them to share it made him want to pump his fists in the air like Rocky.

So when Tanner finally took a breath and nodded, Jensen felt like a weight lifted off his shoulders. Nica sighed, as if she felt the same.

Tanner leaned in and laid his mouth over hers, kissing her until she swayed into him. And when Tanner pulled back, Jensen grabbed her shoulders, turned her and kissed her, too.

Her lips softened under his, one hand reaching to thread into his hair as if to hold him to her. When he pulled back, she looked up at him with wide eyes but a smile flirted at the corners of her mouth.

"Come on, Nica." He nudged her in the direction Sal had taken. "Let's go talk to your friend about getting your roommate back."

They walked back the hallway, Jensen noting the eighties décor. It was comforting, in some weird way. Like he was in someone's grandmother's house. Not that he'd known either of his grandmothers, thanks to his bastard father.

The hallway led to a TV room where the only furniture was a flat screen on the wall, a couch, a side table and a chair—all it would hold comfortably. A dining room followed, a dark table with six chairs and a buffet table along the wall.

Tanner faltered for a brief second before he stepped up into the kitchen. Then he walked to the table and held out his hand to Sal the satyr. Jensen smiled just to think the word.

"Tanner Miller. Our mother raised us to have better manners but it's been kind of an off-kilter day."

Sal smiled, his now-adult face scruffy with dark whiskers. He'd pulled off the knit cap and Jensen saw small horns peeking out from his dark curls. His smile widened.

"No problem, son. Help yourself to some coffee."

Jensen stepped up, unable to hide his smile, which Sal returned. "Jensen Miller. Nice to meet you."

Sal stuck out his hand, his shake firm and strong. "You're the mythology buff, aren't you? Can always see it in an *etera*'s eyes. Just don't ask to pet me, kid."

Jensen laughed because it'd never occurred to him. "You'd probably land that hoof somewhere I wouldn't want it."

"Bet on it. Now…" Sal tapped a finger on the table as if calling a meeting to order. "Tell me about this phone call, babe."

Nica repeated the call word for word. Obviously she'd already told Sal about Friday night and the spell the guy had hit him with—which Jensen still didn't remember—because Sal mentioned it in his follow-up questions.

"Since we didn't find the guy in the database, I'm gonna call Cam, see if he can stop by. Maybe he can get you to remember something about the guy that'll help identify him. And we're going to have to tell Tira's mom and yours what's going on."

Nica grimaced. "Can we hold off on that? Just until Monday? The *boschetta* doesn't have any better resources for finding Tira than we do and it will just…set them off."

Sal shook his head. "No can do, babe. I have to tell Daniela. She deserves to know what's going on. Your mother…well, that's up to you. I'll see if I can head off Daniela, tell her we've already got the de Feos working on it and to sit tight. We'll let her know what's going on when we have news. Honey, if we don't tell your mom, she's gonna find out from Tira's mom and you don't want that kind of trouble."

Nica sighed then nodded though she wasn't happy. "I know. It's just…"

"Just what?" Tanner asked.

She turned to him with a frown. "My mom is a bit of a… Well, hard ass is probably the best word to describe her. And she's not big on men. Any men. She'll want me to come home. She'll think I can be better protected there."

Jensen laid his hand over hers. "Will you be?"

"No," Sal cut in. "She won't. She's safest here. Let me call her and Daniela, Nica. You call Cam and update him. Then take a break, lie down a little. You don't look too good, sweetheart."

* * * * *

Nica's temples throbbed and her stomach ached as she set the phone back in the cradle.

Fear for Tira and worry about Jensen and Tanner sat in her gut like a brick as she rose from a chair in Sal's front parlor.

Cam had had nothing new to tell her. He was working with his brother Rio to track down the guy she'd seen the other night but so far, nothing.

All she wanted to do was crawl into a bed and let Jensen and Tanner make her forget everything. Just for a little while. Just until she felt like the ground wasn't wobbling under her feet.

"Nica." Warm and firm, Tanner's hands settled on her shoulders, drawing her back against his chest. "You need a break. Why don't you go lie down for a while?"

Leaning down, he nipped her earlobe, sending shivers through her body and reawakening her libido. How could she even think about sex at a time like this?

"I know for a fact you didn't get much sleep last night."

No, she hadn't. And thinking about why she hadn't gotten much sleep made her body that much hotter.

She turned in his arms, closing her eyes as she wrapped her own arms around his waist and settled her cheek against his chest. "I don't think I'll be able to rest."

"You don't have to sleep. Just close your eyes."

"Will you come with me?"

If they wanted her to rest, the least they could do was help her relax. She wanted them, both of them, to make her forget just for a little while what a mess she'd made of her life at the moment. Every time she thought of how scared Tira must be, her temples throbbed even harder.

If Cam didn't find Tira by Monday, she was going to hand herself over. It wasn't fair for Tira to pay for something Nica must have done, for the mistake Nica must have made to reveal herself—

"Hey." Tanner tugged on her hair, forcing her to look up into his steady blue eyes. "Come on. Bedrooms are upstairs, right? Let's go find one."

Yes, she wanted that. Even if it was only for an hour. "Okay." She turned to look over her shoulder. "Jensen?"

Jensen sat on the couch in front of the window, looking out onto the street. He looked lost in thought but he glanced up at her when she said his name a second time.

"Will you come up too?"

She wanted—no, she needed both of them. She didn't understand why or how that had happened so fast. Probably a combination of fear and anger.

Then again, maybe it was just because of who they were. And how much she'd come to care for them in the past few days. How she loved Tanner's easy smile and Jensen's hard-won grin, Tanner's laid-back intelligence and Jensen's sharp-eyed intuition.

Her breath caught when Jensen shook his head. "I'll be up a little later. I'd like to talk to Sal first."

She bit her lip to stop herself from begging or demanding him to come with them. The man wasn't her play toy, he wasn't her servant.

But he must have seen something in her eyes because he stood and walked over to her. Eyes open, he kissed her, his hands smoothing over her ass in a caress.

"I won't be long, honey. I've just got a few questions." Then he leaned in close to whisper in her ear. "Tanner will keep you busy 'til I get there. But you better save some for me."

Before he could move away, she laced one hand through his hair and tugged, just once. "Don't be long."

His smile was slow but heated up fast. "You won't even miss me."

He held her gaze for another few seconds until he flashed his brother a look. She barely caught Tanner's brief nod out of the corner of her eye. But even if she hadn't, she'd have known what that look meant.

Keep her safe. Keep her out of harm's way. Tie her in knots sexually and make her forget.

Jensen wanted to talk to Sal. Alone. Probably about her. And he wanted her out of the way.

At any other time, that attitude would have pissed her off. Right now, she just wanted to forget.

She took Tanner's hand and led him up the stairs.

* * * * *

Jensen walked back to the kitchen, trying to formulate questions while half his brain wanted to be upstairs making love to Nica.

She'd wanted that too. And the sooner he took care of this, the sooner he could get back to her.

Her friend's kidnapping weighed on her mind. She thought this was her fault. He knew better.

As children, he and Tanner had lived through hell with their father. The sick bastard had beaten them for anything from not making their beds to crying out in the middle of the night from a nightmare. He'd used their mother as a punching bag, didn't matter if he was drunk or not.

To the outside world, he'd seemed normal, maybe a little uptight. But not the monster he and Tanner knew him to be. Until their mother had had enough and shot the bastard dead when they were twelve.

By that time, they'd figured out they weren't the ones at fault. No matter what they did, their dad was going to beat them.

Nica thought this situation was her fault. Jensen knew better. But that didn't mean her friend wasn't in real danger. And Jensen needed to do something about that.

He walked through the house back to the kitchen, where he heard Sal's hooves clicking against the linoleum floor.

A satyr. He was going to talk to a fucking satyr.

How whacked was that? How completely fan-fucking-tastic. Sal had been right. Jensen had been into mythology and sci-fi and fantasy books and movies as a kid. They'd provided an escape for him, the way music did for Tanner.

But now, knowing there were creatures—no, not creatures, *beings*—in the world straight out of fairy tales, it made him realize the world wasn't as god-awful as he'd thought.

There was still magic.

He reached the kitchen and stopped in the doorway, catching Sal in the act of bending down to get something out of a lower cupboard. The guy's stubby little tail twitched.

"What's up, kid?" Sal asked without turning away from his search of the cabinet. "You got something on your mind. Spit it out."

"How much danger is Tira in?"

Sal sighed, reached into the cabinet and pulled out a can before straightening. "I think if whoever's holding her realizes she has power, they won't give her up. And given that they already know about Nica, they'll attempt to get more information out of Tira."

Jensen's back straightened. "Torture?"

Sal walked to the table and hopped onto a chair, his hooves dangling a few inches above the floor. Jensen forced himself to stop staring and look the guy in his eyes. "Since I don't know who these people are, I can't say no to that."

His mother had endured years of torture at the hands of his father. He couldn't stand by and let another woman suffer like that. "I want them to come after me. I want you to put a tracking spell or something on me so that when they take me, you can find Tira."

Sal didn't say anything right away, just sat there staring at him.

"You and Tanner are twins, right?"

Jensen frowned. "Yeah. But what does that have to do with—"

"I know sometimes twins have special abilities, special languages. Sometimes they can even hear each other's thoughts."

Jensen's frown deepened. "What the hell does that have to do with anything?"

"It means you and Tanner may already have the ability to find each other without creating a spell the person holding Tira may be able to sense."

Well hell. He hadn't thought of that. But Sal had. Tanner and Jensen barely talked about their ability with each other. Why did Sal seem so sure he and Tanner could or would communicate like that?

"Now don't get offended." Sal shook his head, a small smile curving his lips. "No one ever told you there's something magical about twins?"

Jensen snorted. "Not in my house."

"No, I guess not."

The even tone of Sal's voice made Jensen's back straighten. He knew.

Jensen stared into Sal's eyes, seeing no pity. Jensen couldn't stand pity. It made him feel twelve again and facing the cops who came to take his mom and his dead father away.

Bigger and stronger than Jensen, Tanner had always taken the brunt of their father's anger. They both had scars from the bastard but that night, that prick had bloodied Tanner's face, something he'd been careful never to do. And their mother had finally—after so many years of abuse—reached her limit.

She'd shot the bastard with his own gun. The gun he'd been threatening Jensen with after he'd told his father he couldn't finish his homework.

Why his mother had picked that night to find her backbone, he didn't know. Maybe she'd realized the strength it would take to get rid of the bastard would cost her more than she could stand and she figured her sons were old enough to take care of themselves. And her, as it turned out.

Neither Jensen nor Tanner had ever asked her. But that night she'd ripped the gun out of their father's hand and shot him with it. Right after he told her he'd kill her when she wouldn't give it back.

Jensen had made the call to the cops. And when they'd gotten there, they'd taken one look at Tanner and rushed him and their mom into an ambulance.

But they'd treated Jensen, who had no visible wounds, with kid gloves. As if he'd been psychologically damaged.

He'd absolutely hated that.

He and Tanner didn't talk about their father. They barely talked about their mother. Both were gone. And they'd survived.

But Sal knew the story. And probably, so did Nica. And she hadn't seemed to treat them as anything other than regular men.

Then again, she was pretty extraordinary.

"She knows?" He had to make sure.

Sal nodded, still no pity in his gaze, only calm respect. That, more than anything, served to calm Jensen's racing heart. "She won't say a word until you do though. So I suggest you and your brother spill your guts."

Just thinking about exposing themselves like that—

Well, it wouldn't even come close to what Nica had to hide on a daily basis, would it?

Jensen nodded, though he didn't know what he was agreeing to. Yes, they should tell her. But first, they had to find Tira. And Jensen had an idea about that.

"I need to go home."

"Really?" Sal asked though he didn't look at all interested in what Jensen needed to go home for.

"So whoever took Tira can come for me."

Sal just stared at him so he pushed ahead.

"You're right about the twin bond Tanner and I share. We haven't used it much lately but if I get taken, he should be able to find me. Or at least the general area. I'm assuming you'll be able to get backup for Tanner. He's good with his hands. Don't think he can't defend himself—"

"If they use magic against him, like the spell they used on you…" Sal shook his head. "He'll be a walking target. He'll get in the way."

"And you don't have some spell or whatever you can lay on him to make him immune?"

"No such spell, kid. You're either immune to magic or you're not. And there aren't that many immunes wandering around."

"Tanner won't want to be left behind. Not with me missing. And as soon as I leave he's going to know. I was kind of hoping to give them time to get, uh…"

Sal lifted one eyebrow. "Lost in each other?"

That was a good way to put it. "Yeah. Lost enough that I can get a decent head start before he realizes I'm gone."

Because if Tanner had any inclination of what Jensen was going to do, he'd want to go too. And one of them needed to stay behind with Nica.

Sal nodded, though to what, Jensen couldn't tell. "You sure you wanna do this, kid? From what Nica told me about the spell laid on you the other night, you might not come out of this with all your parts intact."

"You know my background. You should know, too, that I'm not willing to stand around and let an innocent woman be hurt when I can possibly do something about it."

Sal's smile lit up his face. "I like you, kid."

"Enough to let us keep seeing her when this is all over?"

Jensen figured Sal had the power to erase their memories at the snap of his fingers. Nica had said she'd screwed up the spell the other night. Sal wouldn't make that mistake.

Sal's smile disappeared as fast as it had appeared. "Not up to me, Jensen. Nica has…responsibilities. It's not my place to tell you what they are. And I can't honestly say she should give them up because of you two. No matter how you all may feel about each other."

"You don't find our relationship—perverted?"

Sal snorted, more disgust than humor. "Kid, you ain't seen perverted until you've met the Roman deities. They make you look like a choirboy."

Jensen blinked. Deities. Had he really said deities? As in gods?

His brain clicked like a broken record for several seconds. "Did you… Do you mean…"

"Don't hurt yourself, kid." Sal laughed. "There's a lot about the world you don't know. Try not to worry about it now. You really sure you want to do this?"

No. "Yes."

"Then you better get the hell out of here."

* * * * *

Tanner felt tension radiating from Nica's body like heat as he led her up the stairs.

She gripped his hand so tight, his fingers began to throb. And she kept looking over her shoulder as if Jensen would suddenly appear and follow them upstairs.

He wasn't sure what Jensen wanted to talk to Sal about. But Tanner had a feeling he wasn't going to like whatever Jensen was planning. And his brother was planning something.

Tanner just couldn't figure out what. He found it hard to read Jensen as well as he used to. As they'd gotten older, it'd been tougher to find that sense of knowing what the other was doing and where they were.

"Tanner?"

Dragging himself out of his thoughts, he realized Nica had stopped. The room she'd taken him to was dark but he clearly saw a bed behind her and the worried look on her beautiful face.

So much worry.

His muscles tensed with the need to wipe that look off her face. The hand not holding hers balled into a fist as fast-building emotion ate at his gut.

After the hell of childhood, he'd learned to keep his emotions to a steady simmer, never letting any of them come to a rolling boil. Nothing good ever came from an excess of feeling. Hell, his parents were the poster children for that one.

So he'd banished anger and fear from his life. And, he realized, severely crippled his ability to love.

Until he'd met this woman.

Staring down into Nica's dark eyes, he saw a woman who wouldn't settle for lukewarm. She was all heat wrapped around a huge heart. A heart he wanted to claim.

He let that simmering emotion rise, battling against his instinctive reaction to shove it back. Let it heat until he felt it all through his body.

Then he kissed her.

He kissed her hard, his lips working hers open so he could get his tongue into her mouth. His hands gripped her hips and pulled her tight against his erection, throbbing already.

If he'd taken her off guard, she caught up fast. She tilted her pelvis into his, rubbing against his cock, making him groan with the powerful rush of desire that hit him squarely in the gut.

This wasn't just sex anymore. At least not for him.

His once-stunted emotions tangled into the mix now, dragging him into a deeper connection with her. One he didn't want to dig his way out of.

One hand laced into her hair, tipping her head back so his lips could work their way down her neck until they met her shirt collar. Without thought, he slid his hands to the hem and ripped it over her head, settling his lips back on hers the moment the shirt was gone.

He kissed her as his hands settled on her breasts, kneading them, working the tight nipples between his fingers. Nica groaned and pressed into him, her hands gripping his shoulders, as if he might pull away.

He wasn't going anywhere. And neither was she. He'd make damn sure of it. And when Jensen joined them, they'd fuck her senseless so she'd have no desire to leave them. Ever.

Moving his hands to her hips, he lifted her off the ground then began to work her tight jeans off her hips with one hand. It wasn't easy but he persevered until he had her naked.

Their tongues dueled as her legs wrapped around his waist. Her fingers scratched at his scalp, pulled his hair. She nipped at his tongue then sucked on it, her breath coming hard and fast as she kissed him.

This wasn't going to be slow and easy. Already he felt his cock tighten painfully behind his jeans, throbbing.

With one hand, he ripped open his jeans and turned to put her back against the wall. She moaned, her hands tightening in his hair, her hips tilting farther. Encouraging him.

He didn't need much. As soon as he got his cock free, he thrust into her. Hard. All the way to the base and she took him like she was made for him. Hot and wet.

Her sheath sucked him in then tightened around him like a fist, milking him. He pulled out, the friction sending bolts of sensation chasing through his system, then shoved back in.

She moaned into his mouth and slammed down on him, so hard he was worried he'd hurt her.

"Nica, baby, I don't want to hurt you. Slow down."

"You're not going to hurt me, Tanner. Just fuck me. I need you."

And he needed her, so much it'd be scary if he let himself think about it. But right now, all he could think about was making her come.

So he did what she wanted, what she'd begged for. Hard and fast, his hips pounding against hers. There'd be time for slow later, when he and Jensen would drive her insane with pleasure. Now, though, he'd make sure she didn't lack. For anything.

And from the sounds she was making, she didn't.

He watched her eyes, glazed with pleasure. Saw her lips swollen from his kisses. He thrust even harder and caught his breath on her cries of ecstasy.

"Tanner, oh gods. Please."

Hips pumping, he felt her contract around him just before she came.

God, so fucking tight.

Her arms clutched him close as she spasmed around him, milking him until he gave in to his own climax.

Still holding her tight against him long seconds later, he leaned his forehead against hers and just breathed. Her arms still tight around his shoulders, her warm breath brushed against his neck.

He should've felt more relaxed. Less stressed.

He didn't.

Something was…wrong.

"Tanner?" Nica's voice whispered across his senses.

He shook his head at the question he heard in her voice. Lowering her to her feet, he tried to throw off the growing sense of impending doom.

Nica wound her arms around his waist and laid her head on his chest. He was tall enough that her head fit under his chin, the tips of her hair brushing against his stomach.

She seemed much smaller standing there, much weaker. But he knew she had a strength that could put the strongest man to shame.

God, he loved her. He opened his mouth to tell her but closed it without speaking the words. Not yet. It wasn't the right time. Not with this sense that he was missing something.

Running his hand through the silky mass, he dropped a kiss on her head. "I'm fine, babe."

"No, something's wrong. What's going on?"

Good question. What the hell was going on? And where the hell was Jensen?

* * * * *

Jensen left Sal's and headed back to his own house as fast as he could.

Now that he'd decided on a course of action, he was committed to it. But damn, he was worried.

Not for himself. He could handle himself.

But he'd left without telling Tanner. He felt as if he'd betrayed his brother. Which was asinine.

They had no secrets, but they didn't live in each other's pockets. They might live together but they led their own lives.

Yeah right. You're pussies, both of you. Living together like perverts, screwing the same woman at the same time. You're degenerates.

It was exactly what dear old Dad would've said had he been there. Jensen heard him as clear as if the bastard was standing in front of him. The man had had an opinion on everything, most of it biased and hateful.

Tanner had learned how to tune him out. Jensen never could. He'd always heard every damn word.

They'd been lucky their lifestyle had never interfered with their business. It almost had, when he'd been stupid enough to fall for the wrong woman. Tanner had known Penny was bad news. Jensen hadn't wanted to see it.

And he'd nearly brought down their company in the process. If Tanner hadn't been able to minimize the damage her vicious gossip had done, they could've lost everything.

And it would've been his fault for letting it get out of hand.

They'd known—from the first time they'd shared a woman in college—they'd known what they enjoyed would never be accepted by society. They'd known they had to be careful.

Yet they were arrogant enough to want it anyway.

Their friends knew. Their friends had boatloads of their own sexual peculiarities. Casimir's love of restraints. Adrien's threshold for pain. Hell, Daniel's preferences alone would keep a psychiatrist busy for the next fifty years.

Which was probably why the group of them got along so well.

It also explained why he felt as if he was betraying Tanner. Because he knew he'd feel the same if Tanner did this without telling him.

Which didn't matter now because he'd reached home.

Parking on the street, he jumped out of the car and hurried to the house. If anyone was watching—and he sincerely hoped they were—maybe they'd think they'd better act fast. Grab him now before he left again.

Could they be waiting in the house? Or on the street?

Jensen forced himself not to look around as he reached the front door and let himself in. He closed the door behind him but didn't lock it, then made for the kitchen. He hadn't really had a plan, more a general idea.

And now—

A breeze ruffled the hair on his shoulders and he turned.

Only to have darkness swallow him.

Chapter Seven

Nica left the tiny bathroom attached to the bedroom and found Tanner sitting on the bed, tapping one foot to a beat only he heard.

An impatient beat if his expression was anything to go by.

His gaze snapped to hers and he stood, holding out his hand.

"Something's going on with Jensen. We need to go downstairs."

Fear made her breath catch and she grabbed Tanner's hand. "What is it?"

"I don't know but I think he might have done something stupid. I think that's what I've been feeling. We need to find him. Right now."

She didn't question as they hurried down the stairs, Tanner practically dragging her along after him. She didn't care.

"Jensen!" he called out before he hit the first floor. "Jensen, where the hell are you?"

They didn't find anyone in the front rooms and Nica's anxiety ratcheted up another notch.

When they reached the kitchen, Nica already knew Sal wasn't going to tell them anything good.

The *salbinelli* sat at the table, drinking a cup of coffee, watching as they stormed into the room.

Tanner stopped dead in the doorway and started to swear. "Son-of-a-fucking-bitch. Why the fuck did you let him leave?"

Sal lifted an eyebrow and took a sip of coffee. "I'm not his keeper. And neither are you. Jensen had a plan. A pretty decent one, if you ask me. Which he didn't, by the way."

Nica released Tanner's hand and walked to the table, her heart pounding. "Where did he go, Sal?"

"He went home, hon."

Sal said nothing else and she took a deep breath to stop the torrent of questions building in her brain. "Why did he leave? Why—"

"He went to flush them out." Tanner's quiet, furious voice made her stomach roll. "He left so they'd take him. So he could find out where your friend is being held. So he could play hero."

"Actually," Sal said, "he's expecting you to find him. So you better get over your self-righteous bullshit fast and concentrate. You need to find Jensen."

Her brow furrowed. "What are you talking about, Sal? How is Tanner supposed to find him?"

"Jesus Christ, he's not serious." Tanner's shocked tone drew her attention away from Sal. She saw Tanner go white, saw the fear in his eyes. "He expects me to know where the hell he is, doesn't he? To *feel* it. Fucking hell. I'm going to kill him."

Nica began to understand what was going on but she knew Tanner was having a tough time. If they were going to find Jensen anytime soon, he needed to get with the program. And he needed her to help him.

Tanner could barely see straight, he was so pissed off and scared for Jensen. But his brother needed him to be strong. And so did she.

"Tanner." She cupped his cheek and forced him to look into her eyes. "Tell me what's going on. Just explain it to me so we can figure out what to do."

Tanner started to shake his head but he kept his eyes focused on hers. As if he needed the connection. "When we were kids, we had a bond. We could pick up on each other's thoughts, our feelings. If we went to the mall, we'd be able to find each other. I don't know how to describe it. We just knew. They were like…flashes of images."

"So you should be able to find him now?"

Shoving his hands through his hair, Tanner rolled his eyes and started to pace. "We haven't done this for years. Literally fucking years. Damn him. I knew he was up to something—"

"Yes, you did." She stepped in front of him, halting his agitated pacing, forcing him to look at her. "And that means you know where to find him now."

And they had to. Fast. She couldn't bear to think about Jensen being hurt, about Tira's fear at being held against her will.

They'd lived such a sheltered life before they moved to the city a year ago, determined to have fun before their lives were co-opted by the *boschetta*. And now it was Nica's fault her lover and her best friend were being held by a faceless enemy.

"No, it doesn't." Tanner practically spit the words out through his clenched jaw. "If he'd just told me what the hell he was planning, we might've been able to figure something out—"

"None of that matters now." She held up both hands to stop his next words. "No, Tanner. All that matters now is your ability to find Jensen. And I think I can help with that."

Blue eyes narrowed as he took that in. "How?"

"My healing gift relies on empathy, on feeling what other people feel. I think I can boost your ability to sense Jensen. Our feelings for him are strong and we should be able to find him faster. Together."

"And when we find him, then what?"

"I have a friend we can call on to help with that. He'll help us get Jensen and Tira back. But first, you need to find them. Only you can do that."

A muscle in Tanner's jaw started to tic. Lifting on her toes, she put her lips over it and kissed him, letting just a little hint of her power ease into him. She needed him to calm down so he could concentrate.

His arms immediately went around her, drawing her close. His heart beat against hers, his rhythm elevated. His heat seared into her skin, calming her as much as she wanted to calm him.

"Just so you know," Tanner tugged on her hair until she tilted her face up to stare into his eyes, "I'm gonna beat the shit out of him when we're done with this."

She smiled up at him, knowing he'd never hurt Jensen. At least not permanently. "And I think you're entitled. But let's get him back first, okay? Him and Tira."

"We will. But," he shook his head, the worried look returning to his eyes, "it's been a damn long time since I've done this."

"Then let's make sure you do it right."

Taking his hand, she drew him back through the house to the front room. Sal trailed along, silent except for the clop of his hooves on the hardwood floors.

She pointed Tanner at the couch and sat next to him.

"I'm gonna give Cam de Feo a call." Sal stopped in the doorway behind them. "See if he's free to give us a hand or if he can send Antonin."

Sal disappeared, back to the kitchen, she assumed, as Tanner met and held her gaze.

She held out her hands, palms up. "Give me your hands."

He reached out and took hers. Tension radiated through him like electricity. If he didn't calm down, he'd never find Jensen.

Moving fast, she straddled his lap and kissed him with enough heat to take his mind off what he had to do. He responded immediately, opening his mouth to let her tongue duel with his. Instantaneous heat flared, tempered only slightly by their combined fear.

The man who'd attacked them the other night had nearly killed Jensen. Would he decide Jensen was a liability that needed to be disposed of? Had he walked into a deadly trap?

They had to get to him now.

As they kissed, she felt Tanner relax, and let her senses open to what he was feeling. Her Goddess Gift gave her the ability to heal the body but it also gave her a sense of what the other person was feeling and thinking.

Tanner was thinking about Jensen.

No, that wasn't quite right.

He was thinking *at* Jensen. Calling out to him mentally. Searching for him.

It was like no magic Nica had ever experienced. And she wasn't even sure if magic was the right word. It was more like another sense, like touch or taste, but one he rarely used.

As she kissed him, and as he kissed her back, he let that sense loose, as if he'd been reining it in for so long he had to remember how to work it.

Afraid to break away for fear of breaking his concentration, she focused on comfort rather than arousal, distraction rather than attraction.

And sank deeper into Tanner's mind than she'd thought possible, connected with him in the same way she'd connected with Jensen when she'd healed him only two nights ago.

She saw Tanner's thoughts, caught impressions of his awful childhood, the hatred he still carried for his father, so deeply embedded it tainted every memory of his mother with its stain. She wanted to cry at the anguish he still carried for his mom's death, for being unable to stop the beatings Jensen had endured.

She caught no hint of self-pity for his own injuries inflicted by his father, only a powerful drive to be a better man, to be strong and stable and enjoy whatever life had to offer. And running beneath that, she felt Jensen.

The bond between them almost felt like a rubber band, elastic yet unbreakable, strong and pliable. That bond resided in Tanner just as her *arus* lived in her.

Tanner broke away with an indrawn breath. "Jesus."

Blinking into his wide eyes, Nica knew he'd found him.

"Where?"

"Christ." Tanner shook his head as if to clear it then closed his eyes to concentrate. "He must be in the city, within a couple of miles. Don't ask me how I know, I just do. He's close enough that I can feel him. Jesus, it's like a string that he's tugging on. I even know what direction to go in. I can't see where he is but when we get close, I'll know."

Tanner stood, lifting her easily along with him and setting her on her feet. "Let's go."

"Tanner, wait." She laid her hand on his arm, knowing he wasn't going to like what she had to say. "We need help. You're not equipped to deal with the people we're going up against."

He stiffened beneath her arm and his expression hardened into a determined mask, though he wouldn't meet her eyes. "I'm going."

"I know. We need you to go, Tanner. But we also need help. The man who took Tira and Jensen nearly killed him the other night. With magic. You don't have magic to defend yourself against him."

She stared up at him, willing him to look at her. "Please. I would be devastated if anything happened to you or Jensen. Please don't make this harder than it's already going to be."

Tanner stared at the wall in front of him, feeling Nica's warm hand on his arm, hearing the real fear in her voice.

She was afraid he'd be hurt. That he couldn't protect himself.

And damned if she wasn't right.

He remembered how the man had nearly killed Jensen by flicking his fingers at him. By putting a spell on his brother and stopping his heart. Neither he nor Jensen had any defense against that. Hell, Nica was better equipped to save his brother than he was.

And that sucked. It fucking sucked ass and made Tanner's blood boil.

Which didn't make any goddamn sense because he'd been pissed as hell when he'd realized Jensen had run off and put himself in this danger for exactly the reason Nica had just given him.

"Tanner?"

He took a deep breath and forced back the out-of-control anger he felt building in his gut. That anger scared him. Always had, because it reminded him of his father.

And he'd sworn never to be like his father.

Another deep breath and he finally let his gaze meet hers. And he couldn't hold the anger. Because beneath the fear, he saw an emotion he'd never seen from another woman. An emotion echoed by his own.

It went beyond mere lust to something deeper. More meaningful. He still wasn't ready to put it into words. And he wasn't willing to think about what it meant for the future. Not yet.

Right now, he had to get Jensen and Tira back.

He was the only one who could find them. So that's what he'd do.

"Tanner, I don't—"

"Hey, babe. It's fine." He smiled at her, cupping her soft cheek and dropping a quick kiss on her lips. "I'm not as stubborn as Jensen. I know we need help. So who's the cavalry?"

"I am."

Tanner turned toward the voice. Sal stood in the doorway to the next room with a dark-haired man who threw off an intensity not even a blind man could miss. Built like a bodybuilder, the new guy was a few inches shorter than Tanner but had to outweigh him by twenty pounds. His jeans and tight t-shirt left no doubt as to how much of the bulk was muscle.

Curly dark hair covered his ears but in no way made him seem feminine, and his dark eyes bored into Tanner's as if he could read his mind.

The guy didn't smile but he did move out of the doorway, holding out his hand. "Cam de Feo."

Tanner took his hand. "Tanner Miller. No offense but we need to leave. Jensen will do something stupid if we don't find him soon."

"Sal says you know how to find him."

"Yeah, I can. Just don't ask me to explain how."

The guy almost smiled. "No problem. I'm used to secrets. So tell me, Tanner. Ever use a sword?"

* * * * *

Jensen woke with a nasty headache.

But with his head pillowed in someone's very comfortable lap.

"Oh thank the Goddess, I was so afraid you weren't going to wake up."

The whispered voice was female but he didn't recognize it. Her hands brushed lightly through his hair, as if she could tell he was in pain.

"Are you okay?" Her hand drifted to his shoulder. "Do you remember what happened to you?"

Jensen forced his eyes open as he slowly rose to sit on the hard floor. Blinking, he looked around. A bare bulb on the ceiling revealed an empty room, no furniture, no windows, two doors. One was closed, the other open.

With a little shake of his head, he focused on the woman next to him.

"Tira?"

The blonde beside him lit up like a candle even in the murk of the room. "Yes," she practically squealed. "Oh please tell me you're my hero come to rescue me?"

"Well, I guess you could call me the first wave."

She frowned as if he'd spoken in a language she didn't understand.

Jensen figured that happened a lot with this woman. She looked like the classic dumb blonde—big blue eyes, wavy blonde hair, a D-cup bra and a size 0 waist.

Then her gaze narrowed and he practically saw her brain start to work.

"You're one of Nica's men from the bar the other night. I recognize you now."

"Yeah, that's me. I'm Jensen. Are you hurt?"

She shook her head. "Other than to kidnap me, I've barely seen the man. He's given me food and water and there's a bathroom back there." She nodded toward the open door. "How did he get you?"

"At my home." He didn't want to say anything else in case the guy was listening to their conversation, didn't want to broadcast the fact that others were coming. "Has he said anything to you about what he's going to do?"

Biting her bottom lip, she stared at him as if looking for something, some hint of what he was thinking or feeling. Then he realized she was debating what she should tell him. "I know about Nica. About who she is and what she can do. She told me, Tira."

Her gaze sharpened even more. "She told you everything?"

"Yeah, she did."

"And did you run screaming all the way back to your house?"

His back stiffened at the implied sneer in her voice. "Honey, I didn't run screaming out of Sal's house. I walked to my car and drove home."

She digested that for a second before she nodded, her expression easing. "And why did you go home?"

"I needed to pick up something. Do you have any idea where we are?"

She paused for a moment and he willed her to stop asking questions he couldn't answer without revealing exactly how he got there.

When she shook her head, he couldn't tell if she was letting him off the hook or answering his question. Then she sighed. "I don't know where we are. He knocked me out and when I woke up, I was here. He did say I'd be free Monday. Just not free as in still alive or as in free of this body."

"Well, let's make sure it's the first and not the second."

And that Tanner was able to find them before whoever had jumped him earlier decided they were no longer useful.

Chapter Eight

"You're sure this is the place?"

Tanner nodded. "Jensen's right through those trees, only a couple yards away."

Cam de Feo nodded, his gaze glued to the rearview mirror of the nondescript sedan he drove. He and Tanner sat in the front, Nica in the back, hunched down so no one could see her. Although the tinting on the windows of the car made that pretty much an impossibility.

Cam hadn't questioned Tanner once during the drive. Once they'd started driving, Tanner had closed his eyes and given Cam directions based on his feelings. Turn left, go right, go straight. And with every passing second, the sense that Jensen was closer increased.

Until it was almost like his brother sat next to him. Then he'd opened his eyes and told Cam to stop.

Looking around, Tanner saw trees and a two-lane road stretching out in front of him.

At first, he hadn't seen a house or a structure of any kind. Then Cam had started forward again.

"Cam, what—"

"There's a lane, hard to see it but it's there." He nodded toward Tanner's side of the car. "Someone went to a lot of trouble to make sure no one saw it. If you say Jensen's here, then my gut tells me that path will lead us to him."

"And you believe me, just like that?"

Cam's mouth quirked in the closest thing to a smile Tanner had seen from the guy. "Yeah, I do. Believe me, it's not the weirdest thing I've seen."

Okay, when he put it like that...

"You're clear on your role here?" Cam asked. "I'm gonna go scout. You and Nica wait here. I'll be back in a few minutes to let you know what we're up against then we'll figure something out from there."

Tanner nodded, shifting the hilt of the sword from one hand to the other. The damn thing was heavy, even though the tip rested on the floor of the car. Nothing like the whip-thin rapiers he'd used for fencing in college. And much sharper. "Yeah, we're clear."

Cam looked him in the eyes for a few brief seconds before he dipped his chin once, stepped out of the car…and disappeared.

"Holy shit."

Tanner stared at the empty space beside the car where Cam had stood a second ago. The man hadn't merely walked away. He'd fucking disappeared.

"Jesus, Nica, what the hell?"

A small warm hand fell on his shoulder and started to knead at the sudden tension there. "Cam is *linchetti*. We call them night elves. They have the ability to become shadow, invisible. If there are no spells around the house barring his way, he'll be able to get in the house without anyone knowing, find out where Tira and Jensen are, and get them out using a teleportation spell."

Tanner's mouth fell open for several seconds before he spoke again. "Teleportation. Like on *Star Trek*."

Nica nodded and smiled but her lips trembled. "Yes. But only if the people holding Tira and Jensen haven't erected wards. If they have, he won't be able to get in."

"So we need a backup plan."

"I think that's why you have a sword. Did you really take fencing in college?"

"Believe it or not, yeah, I did. And I won most of my matches. If Jensen was sitting out here, he wouldn't know what to do with this thing."

Tanner wasn't sure he'd actually be able to use the sword with any accuracy but he would use it and hope like hell that he didn't cut off his own damn head.

Nica fell silent then, her gaze searching the forest, watching for Cam's return.

He hadn't had time to switch his gaze from her when he heard her gasp and Tanner looked around to see Cam standing next to the car.

Shit.

"Wards. Lots of them." Cam shook his head. "I can get in but it'll trip alarms. I don't sense any spells strong enough to keep me in or out so I should be able to get one of them out before they catch me but…"

"Then go in, get Tira out," Tanner said. "And while they're scrambling, I'll go in and get Jensen."

"No, Tanner. You can't. You'll—"

"Nica." Tanner turned to face her. "I'm not leaving without him. Jensen and I know how to fight."

"Not against magic." Fear made her eyes wide. "If that guy throws a spell at you, you could die."

"Then I better be fast and quiet. And if anything happens, we have you to patch us up."

If there was anything left to patch up.

"Tanner—"

Reaching over the seat, he cupped the back of her head and pulled her forward to kiss her. Quick and hard. She fought him, shaking her head, then kissed him back.

When she pulled back, she looked him straight in the eyes. "Don't do anything foolish. Get in and get out. I want you both back."

Tanner smiled at the passion in her voice. "Honey, you won't be able to keep us away."

* * * * *

Jensen blinked when a dark-haired guy suddenly appeared in the room with him and Tira.

Before he even knew what he was doing, he jumped to his feet and stepped in front of Tira.

The guy didn't come any closer. "You must be Jensen. I'm Cam. I'm gonna get Tira out of here. Your brother's coming for you. He should be here any minute. But I gotta get Tira out of here now before they see me."

Jensen turned to find Tira getting to her feet. "Can't you take us both?" she asked.

The guy shook his head. "Spur of the moment. Not enough power."

Hearing footsteps thundering outside the door, Jensen grabbed Tira and practically shoved her at the guy. "Take her. I'll be fine."

"No, wai—"

Tira vanished into thin air along with the guy.

Jensen had two seconds to stare at the empty space in front of him before he realized the door was opening.

Flinging himself against the wall behind the door, he hoped like hell to gain a few seconds of surprise and jump his captor before the guy knew what hit him. Otherwise, the guy could just paralyze him with a spell.

The door flew open, nearly hitting Jensen in the face but he pushed it away and threw himself at the figure in front of him.

Jensen hit him mid-back and tackled the guy to the ground. He knew he had one chance to incapacitate his heavier opponent and he tried to get his hands on the other guy's head and smash it into the floor.

But damn if the guy didn't turn his head at the last second and twist out of Jensen's grasp. Catching hold of Jensen's shoulders, the guy tossed him across the room so hard, Jensen hit the wall.

His ears rang and he shook his head to get his brain to drop back into place. Something wet trickled out of his ear but Jensen pushed himself off the floor and ran straight at the guy again. He expected to get hit with a spell at any moment, to feel his heart seize in his chest.

Nothing happened and he hit the guy's stomach with his shoulder, knocking the air out of him. But Jensen didn't have a chance in hell of wrestling the man to the ground unless he was smart.

And the way the guy started to batter him with his cinderblock-hard fists, Jensen knew smart wasn't going to be enough. He got in a few decent punches, making the guy's head rock back once or twice, but Jensen couldn't take much more abuse.

His head swam, his stomach rolled and pain shot through his entire body as his captor landed blow after blow.

Barely able to maintain his feet, Jensen heard more pounding and figured it was his heart about to burst. At least Tira was safe.

Nica would be relieved—

"Jensen, drop!"

Tanner's voice sounded behind him and Jensen didn't hesitate to obey. He dropped.

The guy released him, whether in surprise or because he figured Jensen was no longer a threat. Jensen had no idea. But when he looked up from the floor, he saw what looked like a long blade sticking out of his captor's chest.

The guy looked shocked as shit. His mouth dropped open and a rush of air escaped, followed by a stream of blood as he coughed.

Following the line of the blade, Jensen found Tanner on the other end of it, holding the hilt, his expression hard and determined.

Holy hell, Tanner had just killed this guy with a sword.

With a yank, Tanner pulled the sword out and the other man fell to the floor near Jensen.

Leaning over, Jensen turned the guy's face toward him. "Who are you working for?"

The man opened his mouth but no sound came out.

"Tanner, we need to find out who he was working for. He's going to die if we don't get him help."

"Nica's in the car." Tanner reached down for Jensen and pulled him to his feet. "Let me—"

"No, I'm right here."

Jensen looked over his shoulder to see Nica hurrying into the room. Her worried gaze traveled over both of them, a little gasp of distress escaping as she took in his injuries.

"Jensen—"

"Babe, I'm fine. He doesn't have a lot of time and we need to know who he's working for."

Her gaze lingered for another few seconds, her eyes dark with worry. Biting her lip, she moved to kneel beside the dying man on the floor.

Jensen watched as she laid her hands over the man's chest, his mouth dropping open as a blue glow enveloped her hands.

When the kidnapper lifted his hand toward Nica, Tanner pushed Jensen behind him and lifted the sword, pointing it at the guy's neck.

"Tanner, it's all right," Nica said as she took the man's hand. "He's too far gone. I can do nothing for him."

"Tell us who you're working for," Tanner demanded.

"It won't matter," the man said, his voice weak and breathy. "You won't find her. My death is only a temporary setback. She won't stop. All I can say is good luck."

Nica drew her hands away from the man with a gasp, the glow vanishing as if it'd never been there. Then she reached out and put two fingers against his neck.

"He's gone." She stood, wiping her hands on her jeans, staining them with the man's blood.

She turned back to Jensen, fear and grief and anger all showing in her dark eyes and the tight line of her mouth. Standing in front of him, she lifted her hands to his face and immediately some of the pain slipped away.

He raised his hands to put them over hers. "Come on, babe. I'll keep 'til we get you out of here."

Looking over her shoulder, he saw Tanner staring at the dead man.

Hell, they all needed to get out of here.

"Guess you knew how to use that blade after all."

Jensen turned to see the guy who'd taken Tira from the room standing behind him, his hand outstretched. "Cam de Feo. You must be Jensen. I suggest you get the hell away before this guy's boss gets here to investigate. Take Nica and Tira home."

"What about you?" Tanner asked.

"I'm gonna clean up the mess, see if I can learn a little something about the kidnapper, maybe get a lead on who he was working for or with. I'll be in touch tomorrow. Tanner, take the sword home with you. Just in case."

Tanner nodded and reached out again for Jensen. "Come on, bro. Let's get the hell out of here."

* * * * *

The car ride was mostly silent.

Nica and Tira sat in the backseat, Nica's arm around her friend's shoulders. She'd opened her sense of empathy to take some of Tira's fear but Tira hadn't been that frightened. Or maybe Nica was too worried about the brothers in the front seat to pick up anyone else's feelings.

They couldn't shield their feelings from her completely but they'd both shut down part of themselves. Probably so one twin couldn't pick up on what the other was feeling. They'd had years to build those walls, to hone them. Even if they didn't consciously realize what they were doing, their mental blocks still worked.

She didn't like that she couldn't read them. In fact, she hated it. She needed to get them cleaned up and into bed.

They'd already decided they would all spend the night at Sal's. Hopefully Cam would be able to figure out who the kidnapper had worked for and Cam and his brothers would be able to take care of the problem.

But there was still the problem of how to protect Jensen and Tanner. And the fact that tomorrow she was expected to take her mother's place in the *boschetta*.

And leave behind these men forever.

* * * * *

Nica didn't expect to find her mother in Sal's living room.

Like a bulldozer at full speed, Carmina Donato made a beeline for her as soon as Nica walked in the door. Her mom wrapped her in strong arms and crushed her against her chest.

Her mom's very real fear nearly suffocated her.

"Niccola, are you okay?"

"I'm fine, Mom. Everything's fine."

"No, you're not." Her mom's gaze narrowed on hers, and Nica forced herself to hold that gaze. "I know what's going on but don't blame Sal. Tira's Aunt Lais had a vision. We need to get you both back home—"

"No." Nica took a step back and out of her mom's arms, closer to Jensen and Tanner, who she felt behind her. "I'm not leaving. Not right now. I'll be there tomorrow. I just need…some time."

Her mom's gaze shot to the brothers and narrowed even further.

Carmina Donato didn't like men on the best of days, but Nica knew her mom had her reasons for being wary. She'd been hurt—crushed, according to some—by her father's rejection and abandonment before Nica turned two. He'd wanted the woman he loved to forsake the *boschetta* and dedicate her life to him and their child.

Carmina had refused and paid with her heart.

Nica had often prayed to the Great Goddess Uni for her father to return, for her mom to turn some of her considerable focus away from *boschetta* business and Nica's training, toward simple family things, like baking cookies and taking Nica to soccer games or softball practice.

None of the *boschetta* children had been allowed to play organized sports. They took too much time away from their studies. They'd all been homeschooled and had received diplomas. But math, English and science hadn't been their major subjects.

They'd been expected to excel in spellworking, herbalism and mastery of their Goddess Gift.

Nica had been raised to believe her only purpose in life was to take her mom's place in the *boschetta*, to serve her people as a healer and to keep the old traditions alive.

Her mom's lips parted as if to say something then shut. And when she looked back into Nica's eyes, Nica saw something flash in her mom's eyes. Something like regret.

"Fine," Carmina said. "I'll expect you tomorrow. Tira, your mom would like you to come home with me. She wanted to come but," her gaze flicked to Jensen and Taylor for a brief second, "you know that was impossible. But she is anxious to see you."

Then her mom did something Nica never expected.

She held out her hand first to Jensen then Tanner. "Thank you. Sal filled me in on the situation and I just wanted to express my gratitude for your help. My daughter means the world to me and...well, I appreciate everything you've done for her and Tira."

"We're just glad everything turned out all right, ma'am." Tanner's respectful tone as he took her mom's hand made tears form in Nica's eyes. She had no idea why. "I'm sorry we had to meet under these circumstances. And we hope to see you again."

Nica's breath caught at the implication behind Tanner's words. He knew what her mom expected her to do tomorrow, knew they would try to change her mind about cutting them out of her life. As her mom had done to her dad.

Nica didn't want to be her mom.

She wanted—

Her mom startled her by hugging her tight and laying a kiss on her throbbing temple, easing the pain there. Then Carmina smiled at her, gathered up Tira and left.

The clop-clop of Sal's hooves announced his arrival and she looked at him rather than meet the gazes of her two men.

"Tanner, why don't you give me that sword. I'll get it cleaned. And why don't you all head up for showers. Jensen could use a little patching up, Nica. Take them up and take care of them."

* * * * *

Jensen still felt a little rattled by the pummeling he'd taken.

And he was pretty sure he had a fractured rib. But that didn't stop him from pulling Nica into the surprisingly large bathroom on the second floor and starting to strip her.

He needed...something. To feel her against him, to take comfort from her presence.

To thrust his suddenly aching, hard cock into her and make her come.

Behind her, Tanner closed the door and pulled his own clothes off before starting the water in the walk-in shower, more than big enough to hold three people.

Nica stood there, watching him out of wide dark eyes. He had no idea what she was thinking.

Maybe he didn't want to know.

As her bra and panties hit the floor, Tanner's hands settled on her shoulders, drawing her back against his chest, allowing Jensen to remove his own clothes.

Then Tanner watched as Jensen stepped into the shower and reached out to draw Nica in after him.

As the hot water hit his back, soaking his hair and easing tight muscles, Jensen wrapped his arms around Nica and sealed his mouth over hers.

Sighing into his mouth, she slipped her tongue between his lips, stroking and licking and making his heart pound and his blood sizzle in his veins.

His hands slid over her wet skin, molding her curves to his tense muscles. The feel of her, more than the heat of the water, began to ease that tension but created an entirely different one.

He sank into the kiss, cleared his mind of everything but the taste of her and the stroke of her fingers as she kneaded tight muscles. Various tiny aches and pains started to disappear and, with a groan, he left her mouth and dropped to his knees, kissing his way down her body. He reached her breasts and sucked one tight nipple into his mouth. She gasped but the sound was cut off as Tanner turned her head to take her mouth.

With his hands on her hips and hers now in his hair, Jensen focused on teasing her. He was no empath but he knew Nica had way too much on her mind. He wanted her to focus only on him and Tanner, on how they made her feel.

He didn't want her to think about what happened later. Hell, *he* didn't want to think about what happened later.

Right now, all that mattered was her.

He licked at her nipples, lapping at the water on her skin, then sucked the pebbled flesh into his mouth. Her hips thrust forward and she shuddered between them. He wanted to continue down her body, kiss a path straight to her clit. But his need to be inside her body, to pound into her, overruled.

As he rose to his feet, Tanner lifted her off the floor and braced her against his chest as Jensen wrapped her legs around his waist and thrust straight into her wet heat.

She cried out as he sank deep, her tight sheath clenching around him. Her gaze locked on his as he began to move, her arms wrapped around Tanner's neck. Tanner had his face buried in her neck, nipping at the delicate skin there while his hands cupped her breasts, fingers and thumbs pinching her nipples.

Her expression ecstatic, she drew in shallow, panting breaths then tilted her pelvis toward him, sliding on him as he rocked into her. She trusted them to hold her, not to drop her. To give her what she needed and tip her over the edge into paradise.

She was almost there, almost ready. She moaned, the soft sound making Jensen's hips jerk forward. He had no warning as he started to come, just the sensation of intense pleasure shooting through his cock and into his body.

He cried out, his hips banging against her. He'd nearly spent himself before he heard her gasp with her own release and knew she hadn't had enough.

Pulling out, hearing her protesting moan, he set her on her feet, pulled her out of Tanner's arms, knowing Tanner would understand.

As soon as he put his mouth over hers, he lifted and held her against his chest as Tanner grabbed her hips. And with one hard thrust, Tanner pumped inside her, shooting her straight into another orgasm.

Her body shuddering as he held her, Jensen felt Nica give herself over as Tanner relentlessly pushed her higher. Her moan made him press her closer, holder her tighter.

Suspended between them, she trusted them to hold her as the water washed over their naked bodies.

* * * * *

"So, sweetheart. You have a decision to make."

Nica walked into the kitchen, feeling guilty about the sleep spell she'd worked over the brothers, guilty about the danger she'd inadvertently put them in.

Heartsick over the decision she had to make. Which wasn't much of a decision.

She dropped into a chair at the table and Sal pushed a cup of steaming hot chocolate in front of her.

"You're going to have to wipe their memories." That was the one thing she knew for certain. "I don't think I can work the spell correctly."

"Yeah, well, whether I do it or someone else does, we have a problem with that."

In the middle of taking a sip of Sal's decadent hot chocolate, she frowned and set the mug down. "What do you mean?"

"I mean, if we wipe their memories, Tanner will never be the same. He killed a man today. That puts a mark on your soul. If he doesn't have the opportunity to work through that with the full knowledge of what he did and why, he'll live his life wondering why he feels this black hole inside him."

Sal's expression softened as she felt tears rush into her eyes. She blinked them back but there were too many to contain.

Sal wrapped his hand around hers, still cradling the mug. The warmth of his hand matched that of the mug. "Babe, the situation doesn't have to be this dire. You know what your options are. If you ask me, there's really no choice."

"I know, the *boschetta* comes first—"

"Oh for fuck's sake, kid, get a grip."

Her eyes widened at the heat in Sal's voice.

"Sal, I'm sorry. I don't—"

"Niccola, listen to me." His tone had softened but not by much. "If you walk away from those two men, do you think you'll ever forget them?"

She didn't have to answer. He had to be able to read her answer on her face.

"Do you think," he continued, "if you shut yourself away from the world and live like your mother that you will ever be happy?"

"No." The word could barely be heard over the tick of the clock on the wall and she forced herself to say it again. Louder. "No."

Now Sal smiled. "Then do something about it. The *boschetta* has cut themselves off from the rest of the world. They've almost become obsolete but our civilization needs them more than ever. But we need them to function in the real world. Yes, the *streghe* need to maintain a connection to the old ways. But if they don't integrate the old ways into the new world, neither will be able to function and the *boschetta* and our people will fade and fail."

"And you think I'll be able to bridge that gap? To make thirteen women who have lived their entire lives a certain way decide their way isn't right? Sal, I'm not my mother. I don't have her strength—"

"Nica, you're handling two strong men. The *boschetta* doesn't stand a chance."

* * * * *

Jensen woke and instinctively froze, waiting for the pain to hit. There was none.

Opening his eyes, he stared at the unfamiliar ceiling for a few seconds, his brain running through what had happened. Yesterday? Today?

He turned and saw Tanner still asleep on the other side of the king-size bed.

Not at home. They were in Sal's house. And Nica was gone. Again.

Trying not to wake Tanner, he sat on the edge of the bed, naked. He looked around and spotted his clothing, folded on a chair by the bed. They looked clean.

Maybe, in addition to satyrs and witches, there really were little cleaning fairies. He wondered if he could hire them to do their house.

Shaking his head at the absurdity of his thoughts, he slid off the bed, dressed—hell, someone had pressed his boxers, for Christ's sake—and headed downstairs.

He headed straight for the kitchen, which seemed to be Sal's favorite room. But the little horned guy wasn't there and neither was Nica.

Glancing at the clock over the stove, Jensen noted the time. Six twenty three a.m.

Hell, they'd slept the night away.

And Nica was gone.

An ache caught him in the chest, having absolutely nothing to do with the beating he'd taken yesterday. The thought that he might never see her again made him want to punch something.

Movement in the backyard caught his eye. Sal crouched on the ground in front of one of the garden beds, deadheading flowers, his goat legs visible in all their glory.

Jensen knew he wasn't out there flaunting his stuff. If Sal didn't want to be seen, he wouldn't be.

Backtracking to the next room, Jensen opened the door and stepped out into the warm July morning. It'd be in the high eighties later today but now it was comfortable.

He walked into the backyard, mostly shaded by a huge oak except for the strip along the side where Sal had a jungle of plants growing.

Jensen recognized tomatoes, peppers, basil, oregano and roses. There was a hell of a lot more than that but Jensen had trained people on the payroll to handle landscaping.

"Is she coming back?"

Jensen didn't bother to beat around the bush. Sal wasn't that kind of guy.

Sal sat back on his haunches and looked up, his face giving away nothing. "I honestly don't know. She's got a lot to deal with. She's carrying a hell of a lot of expectation on her shoulders. And she's fighting centuries of tradition."

The weight on his chest got a little harder. "Are you going to wipe our memories?"

Sal stood, dusting off his hide. "Nope. I'm trusting you both to realize there are some things in this world that need to be kept secret."

For Sal to lay the secret of his existence at their feet was a responsibility Jensen wouldn't shirk. And he knew Tanner wouldn't either.

"We know how to keep our mouths shut."

"Yeah, I'm sure you do." Sal tilted his head the side and his gaze narrowed. "Do you love her, son?"

Did he? Hell, they'd only known each other a couple of days.

Did that matter?

Jensen knew what love wasn't. He'd had an entire education in that from his father. And he knew what he thought love should be.

So, "Yeah, I love her. Tanner does too. She's meant to be ours."

Sal nodded, his mouth splitting in a wide grin. "Glad to hear it. Hold fast to that, Jensen. But don't expect a miracle overnight. Give the girl some time. Both of you."

Chapter Nine

The following Friday, Tanner and Jensen sat at the bar at Lacey's.

All week, they'd looked for trouble behind every corner. They'd found none. No one attacked them. No one approached them. Hell, no one except their employees looked at them funny.

It was like the previous weekend had never happened.

They hadn't seen Nica, either.

Jensen hadn't been fit company all week, growling at everyone. Tonight Tanner had practically had to drag his brother by the hair to get him out of the house.

Tanner had known exactly how his brother felt but he'd thrown himself into the business, working late every night until his head literally hit the desk when he fell asleep. And when he wasn't working, he'd been practicing with the sword Sal had told him to keep.

Sal had told them, before they'd left his home last week, that iron swords couldn't be magically corrupted the way other types of weapons, like guns, could be.

Tanner wanted to be prepared. When Nica came back, he'd be ready to defend her.

Two nights ago Jensen had asked him to teach him a few moves. They'd bought a couple of play swords from a toy store and, though they'd felt like idiots, they'd battled in the basement. Jensen learned fast.

Swords weren't anything like fencing rapiers but the basic fighting technique was the same. Tanner remembered more and more of his training from college every time he picked up the sword.

But they still hadn't heard from Nica.

Every time the phone rang, they'd tensed. She hadn't called. They didn't have a cell number for her and her apartment had been cleaned out. They'd checked Wednesday.

Jensen's mouth had gotten a little tighter, his mood a little darker.

Tanner didn't know what Jensen would do if Nica never returned. He knew what he'd do. He'd drink himself into a coma for a full week then he'd hunt her down, throw himself at her feet and beg her to come back to them.

Jensen... Hell, Jensen might implode before that happened. His brother would never go after her. He'd take her loss like a death. It had taken years for Jensen to begin to get over their mother's.

He could lose the brother he knew, the brother he'd fought so hard to keep among the living for so long.

Lacey had given them a sad little smile when they'd walked in. Obviously she knew what was going on. Even Teo's nod had seemed sympathetic when they'd ordered.

They'd held up the bar for a couple of hours, hoping against hope that she'd show up. Jensen barely strung two words together but Tanner struck up a conversation about the Phillies with the two guys at the end of the bar to pass the time.

But it only served to make Jensen's black mood that much more oppressive.

And when the woman approached Jensen, Tanner held his breath, praying his brother wouldn't blow her off like an asshole.

Tanner breathed a sigh of relief when Jensen forced a smile and a brief but polite "No, thanks."

The woman wandered over to Tanner and he tried to hold up his end of the conversation but obviously didn't do such a good job. She made her excuses and headed back to the table with several other women within minutes.

"How long do we wait?"

Jensen's low-pitched question barely reached Tanner's ears. But he heard the resignation in the tone.

"I don't know. I only know I haven't given up yet."

"You never did know when to throw in the towel." Jensen shook his head and finished off his beer. "Always the optimist."

Jensen's sneer made Tanner's blood pressure spike. His hands clenched into fists at his sides. Jensen was itching for a fight and maybe Tanner was finally ready to give him one.

"Optimist enough to know I'm going to kick your ass, little brother."

"Never happen, old man."

"Let's get the fuck outta—"

"I hope you're not leaving yet. I just got here."

Tanner turned as if someone had goosed him in the ass. His eyes widened and his breath caught in his throat at the sight of Nica. Dark eyes flicking back and forth between him and Jensen, she released the lip she'd been biting and tried a small smile.

It lit Tanner's insides like a match to dry kindling and his body responded with a surge of arousal.

He caught himself just before he reached for her hand to pull her against him. "Hey, Nica."

"Hello, Tanner. Jensen."

She didn't move, just stared at them, as if trying to see what they were thinking.

Tanner's brain rioted with questions, none of which he wanted to blurt out in the bar.

She was here. Standing in front of them. So now what? He flashed a look at Jensen and knew he wasn't going to get any help there. Jensen's expression was purposely blank. If she was there only to tell them she'd never see them again, Jensen wanted to be prepared. He understood his brother's reaction. But Tanner was just so damn glad to see her.

"How are you?" She moved a little closer but still didn't touch them.

"We're fine. How are you?"

Tanner thought he might have detected a smile trying to lift the corners of her mouth but her gaze kept flicking to Jensen. And Tanner was going to punch him if he didn't lighten the hell up.

"I'm... Well, I'm not quite sure what I am." She started to bite her lip again then forced herself to stop. "I know... I miss you both."

"And we missed you."

"What about your situation?" Jensen's voice held no inflection but Tanner knew his brother. If he opened his mouth, he had hope she wasn't going to ditch them again.

Tanner's heart started to pound, so loud he figured everyone close to him had to be able to hear it. And he didn't care.

"My situation...has hopefully changed for the better. And I hope to be making even more of a change. See, there're these two guys..." She flashed another look at Jensen and held his gaze even as she reached for Tanner's hand. "And I'm hoping they might want to—"

Jensen stood and covered her mouth with his, kissing her until she nearly bent under his passion. But then she started to give back as good as she got and, for the first time, Tanner felt left out.

Not that he wanted to embarrass her in the bar by flaunting what others would consider an alternative arrangement. But when Jensen stepped back, nearly panting with arousal, Tanner pulled her forward and kissed her just as hard. He didn't give a shit what the fifteen or so people in the bar thought. He only knew she was theirs. And the rest of the world could deal or go fuck themselves.

When he released her, she stared up into his eyes, smiling that beautiful, slow, sexy grin he'd fallen so damn hard for the first time he'd seen it.

"Can we go now?" She nodded as if answering her own question. "I'll explain everything in the car but... I'd like to have you alone—"

"Jensen, get the bill." Tanner grabbed her hand and started leading her toward the door. "And hurry up."

He didn't look back as he hustled her out to the car a block up the street. Nica hurried along beside him, the click of her tiny heels barely audible. He unlocked the car with the remote, opened the front passenger door and lifted her onto the seat sideways. Then he couldn't help himself. He slid his hands up under the skirt of her short, strappy brown dress and let his palms soak in the heat of her silky thighs.

With a sigh, she leaned forward to rest her forehead against his. "Tanner..."

"Yeah, babe?"

"I'm sorry I couldn't come to you sooner."

"I'm just glad you're here now."

"Get the damn truck started and get us the hell out of here, Tanner." Jensen gave him a shove from the side, knocking Tanner away from Nica, who transferred her smile to Jensen.

Jensen cupped her face in his hands and just stared into her eyes. "I want to go home. Now."

Then Jensen slid her around so she was sitting in the seat properly and fastened her seat belt before getting in the back of the SUV.

Tanner slid into the driver's seat with a grin on his face and started for home.

"So tell us what happened, babe," Jensen said, "because once we get home, we won't be talking."

Nica smiled, anticipating a night *not* filled with sleep.

Blessed Goddess, she'd missed her men.

She'd spent literally the entire past five days making her case to each member of the *boschetta*, both separately and together, about how to make the group viable in this century.

"I convinced my mother and the rest of the *boschetta* that to be meaningful members of our community, we need to live in the community, not hidden away, hoarding our gifts. They've been so entrenched in a way of life that may have worked five hundred years ago that they've lost sight of their true purpose."

"And that is?" Tanner asked.

"To make lives better. Not just for those few people who continue to seek us out but to make ourselves known to those who don't. Our people have been losing the connection to the old ways for centuries. Many no longer go to worship. They don't practice magic. They don't tend their Gifts. And every year, we lose a little bit more of our culture and our power.

"The women of our *boschetta* have held on that much harder to everything but we don't live in the community to help those who may need it. I convinced them it's in our best interest to change our strategy."

"And if you hadn't been able to change their minds?" Jensen's low voice hit all her buttons, making her go wet between her legs.

"Then I would have left. Because my concentration would never have been completely on work because half of my soul would be with you two."

Neither man spoke for several seconds then Jensen's arm encircled her from the backseat and Tanner's hand gripped her thigh.

"Nica." Jensen's voice whispered into her ear, electrifying nerve endings and making her sex clench. "We've been miserable without you."

"I can personally vouch for his miserable, babe."

"You weren't exactly Mr. Happy either," Jensen shot back.

"Yeah but I don't mope."

Nica's face began to ache from her smile but she didn't want to stop.

She'd missed them both so badly.

"Neither do I," Jensen said.

Tanner snorted and Nica started to laugh. She couldn't help it.

"Can't you go any faster, Tanner—" Her breath caught as Jensen's hand cupped her breast through the tight bodice of her dress. His fingers plucked at the tight nipple, sending bolts of pleasure straight to her womb.

She moaned, her eyes closing as Tanner's hand tunneled beneath her skirt and made a short but seductive trip up her thigh to the wet heat between her legs.

Panties soaked already, she tilted her hips, trying to get Tanner's hand to slip beneath the wet lace and finger her clit. But he only brushed his fingers over it and retreated. And repeated.

Jensen had a firm grip on her breast, alternately caressing the tip and kneading the aching mound.

Only the sound of their panting breaths could be heard. Keeping her eyes closed, she let herself fall into a state of pure arousal. She felt only their hands on her body, their scent surrounding her.

She barely registered the car stopping but moaned her disappointment when Tanner removed his hand. A rush of air filled the car as he got out but Jensen plucked harder at her nipple and she bit down on her lip to stop from crying out. Still, a strangled sound escaped.

"Shh, baby," Jensen crooned in her ear. "Hang tight. We'll be inside soon."

Her door opened and another rush of warm air filled the car. She looked up as Tanner released the seat belt and Jensen released her. She practically fell in her haste to get out of the car but Tanner lifted her into his arms and turned for the house.

Jensen had the door open for Tanner to walk through and he didn't stop until he reached the back bedroom on the first floor. The one with the huge bed. Which Tanner threw her on.

Bouncing, she started to laugh but her breath caught in her throat as her men started to shed clothing like ducks shed water. Easily and fast.

Neither of them made a sound but the boiling hot look in their eyes made her lungs ache to draw in air. Mesmerized by the perfection of their naked bodies, she could only stare as Jensen flipped her skirt up and ripped off her panties while Tanner pulled her dress over her head. She hadn't needed a bra so she was naked in seconds.

And in the next second, Tanner crawled onto the bed next to her and pulled one taut nipple into his mouth to suckle. The suddenness of the action caused her body to shoot higher into arousal. Her fingers threaded into Tanner's hair, gripping the short strands and tugging, though not to pull him away.

And when Jensen pulled her legs apart and settled between them, she reached for the slatted headboard to hold on.

She did cry out when he slid his hands under her ass and put his mouth over her pussy. His tongue pressed into her slit, lapping at her. Sensations zipped through her body as the men dedicated themselves to giving her pleasure.

Their mouths devoured while their hands caressed. Jensen held her thighs apart, his fingers kneading. Tanner had his hands on her breasts, one plumping, one teasing her nipple.

She let herself sink a little deeper into bliss, knowing she would have been a fool to let these men get away.

As if Tanner had heard her thoughts, he lifted his head and she looked up into his eyes. The expression there made her reach up and pull him down to kiss her. She only ever wanted these two men, only—

She gasped into Tanner's mouth as Jensen moved, rolling her onto her side, plastering her against Tanner's front.

Tanner's erection ground against her mound and she raised her leg to place it on top of his. She needed to be filled, needed to come. Anticipation and a week's worth of angst rose up like a storm inside her. She had to claim these men, her men.

She shifted her pelvis higher, rubbing the tip of Tanner's cock against her clit, the sizzle of impending orgasm making her feel wild, untamed.

With her hand on his shoulder, she forced Tanner onto his back, straddled his lap and impaled herself on his cock mindlessly. Tanner groaned as she sank to his root, her back arching. She started to ride him, setting a fast pace that brought her almost to the edge.

She felt Tanner's restraint in the tightly bunched muscles of his arms as she ran her hands over them, saw it in the clench of his jaw.

He looked into her eyes, the blue of his almost navy with arousal.

Then his gaze flicked over her shoulder and she felt Jensen move behind her, his mouth biting into the sensitive lobe of her ear before he whispered, "Lean down."

She barely understood what his words meant, she felt almost disconnected from everything but the pleasure.

But when Jensen put his hands on her shoulders and started pushing her forward, she followed his lead without complaint. And gasped when silky liquid cooled the tight pucker of her back entrance. Jensen spread the lubricant liberally, the warmth of his body heating the liquid until she panted.

"Jensen, oh Gods."

She knew what was coming. She wanted it, wanted to be possessed by both of her men.

Tanner wrapped his arms around her shoulders as her breasts met his chest then they both lay still as Jensen positioned himself behind her.

Nica forced herself to relax. She wasn't prepared for the sense of fullness or the utter destruction of her sanity that followed when they began to move in wicked synchronization.

She cried out, something incoherent, and heard Tanner soothe her in a low voice as Jensen groaned behind her.

"You're so tight, baby," Tanner crooned. "So hot and smooth. Come, Nica. I want to feel you come all over my cock."

"Fuck, she's like a glove," Jensen growled as he pushed his way back into her ass. "I'm not gonna last. Come on, Nica. Come on. Come."

She didn't want to come. Not yet. She wanted to hang there between them, suspended between blistering orgasm and blissful unconsciousness.

Reaching for her *arus* to help her, she let the magic rise up, let it mingle with her desire and open her to the brothers' feelings.

Their desire consumed her in a rush of heat so devastating, she nearly lost consciousness. She cried out at the sensation, wanting more, dying for more.

Her *arus* extended to encompass the men, heightening their excitement. She felt their heat increase as it mingled with hers, the whole of it creating a supernova climax that exploded through her entire body. Her sex convulsed, clamping around Tanner's cock, making him groan as Jensen let loose with a string of profanity that only made her burn hotter.

Tanner's release mixed with her own and Jensen pumped into her ass, filling her with warmth.

Boneless, she lay between them, unable to move, unwilling to move.

After a few seconds, Jensen slipped his cock free, causing her muscles to contract, setting off mini orgasms again and making Tanner tense beneath her as she squeezed around his cock.

Jensen flopped onto the bed as Tanner turned them, slipping out of her but not releasing his hold on her. With Jensen curled around her back, his breath hot on her nape, and Tanner kissing her with a lazy intensity, Nica smiled.

Reaching behind her, she laced her fingers through Jensen's hair, making sure she had his attention, then leaned back so she could look from Tanner to Jensen.

"Are you sure this is what you want?"

Jensen leaned forward and nipped her neck. "We've never been more sure. We love you, Nica."

"And if you're willing to put up with us," Tanner said, "we're more than willing to make this work, whatever it takes."

"I love you both. We'll make it work. All of it. Because I'm not willing to fail. Or lose either of you. Ever."

The End

www.ingramcontent.com/pod-product-compliance
Lightning Source LLC
Chambersburg PA
CBHW071317130626
46556CB00004B/1642